D1253151

THE FAERY QUEEN'S DAUGHTER

MELISSA MARR

To Charles de Lint,
I wrote this one—my first novel—because you inspired me.
Thank you for friendship & words. If I ever end up in a faery realm, I
hope you'll come with me.

&

To MaryAnn,
This in the world because of you. You're a treasure, & I remain grateful to
know you. Some fine day, I expect you to admit that you've been a faery all
along.

Prologue: in which paths cross

❧❦❧

I vy watched Jonquil's face as the little Ellyll peered out from the foliage around them. The tiny faery's multi-toned skin, like a strange blossom in the dark, made it impossible to truly hide herself Above-Ground.

Most fey were afraid, terrified of the shadows that crept and sent secrets back to the palace. Everything had become so incredibly *wrong*, but if a faery the size of Ivy's hand could risk everything, the mad queen's daughter could do no less.

Ivy stepped closer to the tree and asked, "Do you think the queen is getting any better?"

Jonquil stepped off the edge of the branch, hovering in a sliver of moonlight, wings glimmering and peered into one of Ivy's eyes. "Do *you*?"

"I don't know . . . If she is, why does the Queen refuse to talk to me? " Ivy stopped, her words barely audible under the belling of the hounds. They echoed through the night, terrible long, low calls coming closer. That sound was only a moment's warning before the terror followed.

Jonquil paled.

"*Run*," Ivy said.

The tiny faery's feet touched down on the mossy soil at the base of a nearby tree. Her hand pushed on the knotty wood where a wee door was hidden before darting through a miniature door to the faery realm, leaving Ivy alone in the face of the oncoming horror of the Huntsmen and their beasts.

Ivy's feet barely touched the soil as she leapt over branch and bramble

The earth shook as the Huntsmen's horses came into range. Like a nightmare come to life, the skeletal steeds trampled everything in their path. At this distance, only the eerie green glow of their eyes and the sulfurous clouds of their breath were clear.

Even that scant look was enough. Terror surged into the very air around her.

Ivy scrambled into a tree. *I shall not fear them. I cannot . . . do not fear. I am not the quarry.* She bit down on her lip to keep from whimpering; her knuckles whitened as she clenched a limb.

A crashing rose from the ground, too frantic to be the hounds.

Ivy glanced down, hoping that whatever it was hadn't led the Hunt to her hiding spot.

A mortal man and woman ran into sight, the woman's skirt in tatters, the man's cheek bleeding. The man watched over his shoulder while the woman hoisted a bundle midway up the tree into a hollow, frantically packing leaves and soil in after it.

"Hurry," the man whispered. He tugged the woman's hand so hard she stumbled.

And they were off. Their feet stirred clouds of dust as they ran down the path leading to the nearby mortal village. Without the shadows and the scents of the forest to mask their humanness, they had little chance of escaping the Hunt.

What fool reason would send them into the open like that? Ivy shook her head; mortals seldom made sense.

The Hunt came into view. The hounds were like a black wave under the horse's hooves. Sparks of red flashed in that rolling darkness as the hounds' eyes became visible. Above that awful vision were the Huntsmen themselves, some bare-chested, some armored. They were a strange mix of folk and mortal, plucked from their rightful times to join the Hunt. Sometimes, their armor revealed their era; often, though, trying to focus on any one when they were in motion was like watching a tongue of flame in a roaring fire. Each one was too quickly lost in the mass that surrounded it.

Had things become so bad that the Queen would let loose the Hunt aboveground without sending warning?

They were hers to command, a fierce weapon, but not one released lightly.

Then as swiftly as they'd approached, the Huntsmen shifted course, their thundering hooves veering away from the copse of trees where she hid, following the path the mortals had taken.

Still trembling, Ivy dropped to the forest floor. Even though the Hunt had raced away, dragging their waves of terror with them, she no longer wanted to be Above-Ground. She could pretend they were no more than nursery boggles--harmless to her now that she was older --but her heart hammered still.

The Hunt rides.

Pretending didn't make the terror abate, didn't make the nightmares any less real.

She turned to flee, but then she heard it: an unmistakable cry from the hollow in the tree.

Go. Go before they turn back.

She closed her eyes and took a deep breath. *Maybe it's just an animal. Go.*

The cry rose louder.

It's not my responsibility.

As daughter to the queen, Ivy had shouldered more than enough responsibility in her fourteen years. She didn't need this one, too.

I could still run.

With shaking hands, Ivy removed the handful of twigs and moss the woman had packed in.

Why are they after this?

Ivy lifted the dirty length of cloth and the mortal babe it was wrapped around.

If the queen sent the hounds after him, he mattered to Ivy. The queen of faery might be mad, but she didn't bother with mortals—not unless they were special.

Chapter 1: In which Jack Merry discovers that all is not as it would seem

❧

"Inside the faery hill, they dance to music that plays endlessly, lilting rhythms like the music of the stars in midsummer." Jack Merry grinned at the townsfolk who had paused in the court-yard to listen to his tale while they took their midday meal.

Some of them looked at him, waiting. Even those that didn't look his way were listening.

"Sometimes," he continued, "if you close your eyes at the moment when the sun slides away at night, you can hear their feet as they dance."

And for a moment, he imagined that he *could* hear it—the tramp of dozens of feet moving in time to strange songs. Such music couldn't be made by the crude instruments the farmers strummed on the rare occasion when they remembered to rest. The music would be magical, so tempting that no one would remember to do anything but rejoice. Surely, that would be what live in Faery would be life.

"What else do they do, Jackie?" asked a farmer with a creased face. Like the rest of the people in Hollow Groves, he was weath-erworn and somber.

Sitting in the dusty street, Jack tried to look past the fading wooden buildings and cheerless faces. *What would please them? What will make them stay a little longer to listen?*

"Well, they have feasts the like of which we've never known--long tables covered in silver trays piled so high with sweets that it takes a full day to even see them all." He paused and sighed, picturing it in his mind, layers of white icing-covered cakes and creamy puddings. "They're so happy that they laugh as they twirl round the table. Sometimes, they don't even stop dancing to eat. They just reach out a hand as they swing past the table . . ."

Many of them listened, held rapt as they often were when he spun tales, but some of the townsfolk finished their meals and left, returning to their fields and stores. They didn't say anything, just left. Jack felt like his words lost their magic bit-by-bit as people turned away. He knew it was silly, that magic wasn't real, but he tried.

Keep talking. Maybe a few will linger.

"And the clothes they wear . . ." He shook his head and sighed longingly. "Coats and gowns of spidersilk with dew still clinging to it, just enough that it glitters when they twirl by the giant fires that they tend all through the day and night. It's glorious to see, but it's never the same twice. In fact, they can only wear their coats and gowns one time. You see, they dance so feverishly that after just the one night of dancing, the cloth is too tattered to be used for anything but rags."

Jack wasn't sure where to go next, but it didn't matter. No matter where he wandered with his stories, it wasn't enough. Before he could even try to add another line to the tale, the last of the townsfolk wandered away.

And Jack was left alone.

Again.

⁂

As Jack spun his fanciful tale, Ivy stayed in the shadows,

listening. She could almost hear the revelry in Jack's story, and she swayed as if the rhythm had crept inside her skin. Even after his voice had faded and he sat silently, she could still imagine the music, the laughter. She wished his words were true, but her home hadn't been so lovely in her whole life.

Faery was sick, withering with disease and sadness, just like the queen.

"Ivy!" Jonquil gripped a handful of hair as Ivy had started to dance, and the wee Ellyll was getting tangled in Ivy's long tumble of red hair. The faery girl said, "Give a bit of warning!"

"Sorry!" Ivy edged forward to see which way Jack went. When the people started leaving, Jack became stiller and quieter.

Ivy ducked behind an old barrel, careful not to touch the metal ring that wrapped around it. One could never be sure with mortal-made things. A foolish brush against the wrong stuff and she'd have an ugly burn to explain—proof she'd been where she shouldn't, reason for a lecture. Fields and woods weren't littered with iron the way villages were.

Carefully, she rested her cheek on the wood and waited.

"What are you doing?" Jonquil clutched Ivy's earlobe, her fingers curling around the edge, tickling it terribly.

"Shhh!" Ivy reached up and rubbed her ear, pushing her friend further from it.

In front of her, Jack yanked his cap off his head and shoved his curls back—even though *he* had no pesky Ellyon tickling his ear.

Ivy waited to see if he would go towards the lake or back to the Parson's house. If he went to the Parson's, Ivy would have no more chance to watch him today. That man's house was riddled with iron.

But Jack grabbed his bag off the ground and slumped toward the lake.

Ivy had listened as Jack told his tales to the creatures at the lakeside. They weren't real, but they were a lot prettier than what was real. When he spun stories, Ivy could forget crimson rivers and bone-dry lakes. Jack never spoke of rowan-children struggling to move over earth so foul it began boiling, oozing thick yellow slime. Instead, Jack Merry spoke of the world she wished her home could be, a world where the folk were happy and laughing.

With a nervous catch to her voice, she told Jonquil, "Go on. I'll be along soon."

Then, she headed to the lake.

§ⓐ

AFTER SHE'D BEEN SENT AWAY BY IVY, JONQUIL PAUSED IN THE shadow of a dappled tree. She look around to make sure that she wasn't watched, and then she ducked into a door that not even Ivy knew existed.

"Waited for you, days now." The scorpion-wife clacked her pinchers. "Do you think it so easy then to sneak away to meet you?"

She scuttled further into the burrow where she had been pretending to nest. Bits of something stringy and red squished under her many feet.

Trying not to shudder, Jonquil followed her. For an Ellyllon to go into such a place—

Best not to think on it.

"I'm here." Jonquil tucked her hands into her pockets, fingering the poison-pouches she kept there. It'd be a battle to get them into the scorpion-wife's maw, but if it came down to that or joining the remains on the floor, she'd have little choice. "Ivy's near ready to do something. Tell them."

The scorpion-wife grinned, flashing the fang-like chelicerae on either side of her mouth. "If the young one acts, we will wait. *I* cautioned against it. *I* wanted to act. Assassination is so satisfying." She closed her eyes for a moment, savoring some image that Jonquil was happy not to share. "But the others . . . They have no vision."

The scorpion-wife waved a pincher, like she was swatting a bog-fly.

"Ivy's growing impatient too," Jonquil said. "She knows the folk talk of revolt. She may not support the queen, but she doesn't want her mother to be dead."

Jonquil loosened her grip on the poison in her pocket, but she kept it in the palm of her hand. Scorpion-wives weren't the best at controlling their impulses. "Tell the others to wait just a while longer."

"And if I don't like your plan?" The scorpion-wife scuttled closer again, crowding Jonquil. "If no one ever knew you were here? Little winged thing. Not much bigger than a fly . . ."

Jonquil didn't have sharp edges like the creature in front of her, but the poison in her hand would incapacitate even the healthiest of the creatures. She squeezed a pouch so it puddled in her palm, then she pulled both hands out of her pockets, and held them open before her. The slick green ooze shimmered in the low light. In the other, an unbroken pouch sat like a promise.

Loose poison in the eye. Pouch in her mouth. I can do it.

The scorpion-wife scuttled back three steps. "We will wait. Not forever."

Jonquil backed toward the entrance to the burrow, hands still outstretched.

❧

AS JONQUIL FLEW TOWARDS THEM, DAISY PLUMMETED FROM the branches of the white willow and hovered beside her sister. "Jonquil! Did you hear me? You're late. And why didn't you bring Ivy?"

Jonquil scooped up a beetle and cradled it. "She'll be here."

Daisy zipped back up into the branches to the bird's nest where their sister Clematis had been napping. "You know where's she was going, don't you?" Daisy said.

"No. But I can guess." Clematis grinned like a half-mad cocka-trice. "Ivy's gone off to the same place as always: to stare at her mortal."

The nest shifted as Daisy flopped down. It was sheer foolish-ness to believe Ivy's status would keep her safe from the Queen's madness. "One day, the Queen won't forgive her. One day, Princess Ada will convince the Queen that Ivy's a threat. And then what?"

Her sisters had no answers. They never did. Ivy was their best hope for the future, but she was too young to think about crowns and revolutions.

❦

JACK STROLLED DOWN THE ROAD OUT OF TOWN, PAST THE houses and porches where townsfolk murmured amongst themselves.

"Boy needs to be sent away. He has fey blood." An elderly man shook his finger at the people around him. "No good comes of the wild ones."

They nodded, watching Jack warily. Though they were kind enough, they still didn't accept him at their hearths. They never had. He was fine for a story, a scrap or two when they had plenty, but no one trusted Jack Merry.

Normal boys don't show up out of storms.

In solemn tones, they'd repeat the story of his mysterious arrival. They'd swear the basket on the parson's doorstep was as dry as tinder, despite the terrible storm that night; they'd claim that the long-since-lost blanket wrapped around him that night was as delicate as if it were woven of moonlight. In the telling, they'd convinced themselves that Jack was something Other.

Jack believed none of it.

He was as human as they were. He was ordinary in every way except for being an orphan. They made him extraordinary in their whispers and fears, and the result was that Jack was lonely.

And all he wanted in the world was to have a family or friends.

Widow Stonewell lifted a weathered hand as he strolled by her. She, at least, was kind to him. "Give my regards to the Good Folk, Jackie."

Sure, he'd dreamt it was true, that he was one of them; he hoped, begged, prayed even. Now, he just considered it a good excuse to spin the stories he liked to imagine. If they were going to treat him that way, why not pretend to be what they all thought he was?

"I will." Jack tipped his cap to her.

Then, he continued towards the shore of the lake.

At the lake, Jack leaned against an oak tree and thought of tales to tell the townsfolk. When winter snows lay heavy on the fields, they'd stop longer than those few moments at midday. They'd invite him to sit near the tavern fire; then, he was almost a part of the town.

Almost.

He stared at the sky, imagining what it'd be like to belong, not to be kept at a distance. The girls would giggle and look away. The townsfolk would wink and nod. He'd have a place, and he'd have a future.

A barefoot girl, clad in dark green breeches and a long-sleeved tunic, stepped out of the woods. "Shall I sit with you?"

Without waiting, she sat down beside him and stared out over the water. Though her clothes were cut of a cloth he'd not seen on even the wealthiest families, she sat on the ground as if her clothes were as ragged as his.

"You want to sit with *me?*" Jack stared at her.

She had dark eyes, like a night without stars, and those dark eyes were assessing him as if he were something peculiar—not as the townsfolk did, but as if peculiarity was a wonderful thing.

The girl buried her toes in the soft soil. "I'm Ivy."

"Do you know who I am?" he tried to sound teasing, but he felt the strangest urge to run. Mad as it seemed, he could almost swear he'd seen a deer with those same eyes watching him from the edge of the trees.

Girls are not sometime deer, not even in the stories he made up.

"Oh, indeed, I do know." She nodded rapidly, sending red hair away from her face, revealing features too delicate to be real. Her ink-black eyes widened just slightly.

He wondered if the girl beside him was somehow kin to the woodland creatures that gathered at the lake. He couldn't decide if she seemed more like the deer or the wolves he'd seen in the forests. Whatever she was, she wasn't someone he'd ever seen in the village.

She held his gaze as she pronounced: "*You* are Jack Merry, the so-called son of the faery folk."

Jack swallowed hard, watching her. *She's merely a girl--an odd girl, but a girl nonetheless.* He swallowed hard several times and tried to calm himself.

She leaned so close that her breath was warm on his cheek. "Oh, Jack Merry, are you quite all right?"

Jack could hear a faint ringing of bells, delicate things that in his mind were made of sea glass. Perhaps he'd been too long in the sun--imagining strange girls as forest animals, hearing bells. Before long, he'd be muttering faery legends like the good Widow.

"I'm . . . fine," he insisted. "I'm completely fine."

He leaned back against the oak tree and tucked his hands behind his head to hide their trembling. His voice was barely shaking when he asked, "So, aren't you afraid the fey folk will spirit you off to a faery hill if they come to visit me?"

She laughed--an eerie sound, like a loon's song on a dark night--and the resounding ring of glass bells grew briefly deafening. Then she winked and began pulling items from her satchel.

"Tell me a story, faery boy."

❦

IVY WATCHED JACK WRESTLE WITH THE URGE TO RUN FROM her. He clenched his jaw; he looked around. He swallowed loud-ly.Then, settling his gaze on the lake, he reached up and tugged that horrible cap off his head. He squirmed, but he hadn't run yet.

She prompted, "If we were to go to your faery-hill . . ."

She began braiding a length of rope together with a flowering vine. If he couldn't get past the natural fear mortals seemed to feel around the folk, well, it was all for naught. She'd hoped that all her visits in the guise of deer would help him learn to resist that fear, but here he was looking like he was a heartbeat from flight. It was disappointing, but she wasn't going to give up on him yet.

He was special: she knew it. From the shadows, she'd listened to his tales and remembered the old legends--a mortal who'd tell a tale that *became*. Jack Merry could do that; she was sure. He could change things. He could help her save her home.

Jack began, "Well, inside the hill, the feasts last longer than a human's life. And the tables are always set with silver goblets that gleam like they're filled with moonlight."

He paused, a small smile on his lips.

And Ivy knew he could see the things he'd spoken, see them in his mind as truly as if they'd floated to the surface of the lake in front of them.

She whispered, "Would you go to the faery realm, Jack Merry?"

Jack laughed, quick and fleeting. "Perhaps I have. Perhaps it's why I know these stories."

"You haven't. We both know that, but suppose you *could*. Would you go there, really and truly?" She paused, twisting the intricate knots in her rope. Her fingers were clumsy with excitement and nervousness. It was making the process take far longer than it usually did. "If you were invited, what would you say then?"

Jack lifted one eyebrow. "Aaah, but a mortal can't stay there, and they say that once a person goes inside a faery hill, he'll waste away from wanting once he returns to this world."

Ivy thought of the changes in the realm, trees rotting and waters thick with strange poisons. She shook her head. "They're wrong."

Then, she lifted the vine and whistled, long and piercing.

❧

SUDDENLY, THE WATERS SHIVERED. IN FRONT OF THEM, forming as if from the water of the lake itself, was a great white horse with eyes as green as the moss in the deepest part of the forest and a neck as thick as ancient trees. It drew a deep breath, sides quivering.

Jack blinked. Water didn't solidify into horses. That was simply not how anything worked.

But it stood there, larger than any animal he'd ever seen. Light rippled on its skin, just as it did on the lake's surface. The magical creature in front of him was both horse and water all at the same time.

Ivy hopped up from the ground and walked calmly toward the creature. She stood ankle-deep in the water, held out her hand--palm up--and murmured, "Shhh, now."

The beast huffed a great breath, filling the air with the sweet scent of lilacs, as if objecting. Then, it made a noise that might have been a word but was probably a nicker. Finally, it lowered its head.

Murmuring strange words, Ivy rubbed her cheek against the animal's face, and then she looped the braided vine about his neck.

It stood perfectly still. The only movement was the steady deep breaths it drew, but the sense of barely restrained movement was almost tangible, as if the smallest step would start an unstoppable charge.

And Jack was sure that whatever was in its path would be trampled.

Ivy swung herself astride the water-horse. Holding the end of her vine in one hand, she extended the other hand towards him. As she did, he could see misty shapes of wings unfolding on her back, like the fog in the morning was hovering behind her back. They weren't solid wings, and he wasn't so sure they were ever present, but if he had to swear to the parson, Jack was certain he could say he met a faery at the edge of the lake.

"So what say you, Jack Merry? Will you join me?" Ivy asked.

"You're *real.*" He let out a long breath, before whispering, "It's all real? Faeries?"

"Oh, indeed, Jack, we are quite real." Ivy held up her hand and added, "But there's strife aplenty where I go, and not all fey things are . . . kind."

Her eerie black irises widened so far that if he'd had any doubt that she was something Other, it would've fled in that instant. "Will you trade vows, Jack Merry? Let me take you into the faery realm. Stay with me for three days, and I promise you my full truth on whatever you ask of me by the third eve."

A shiver ran through him as she spoke, but Jack gripped his tattered sack and looked up at her.

'Strife aplenty,' she said.

He looked around at the woods, the lake, the world he knew. Then he turned his gaze to her, a faery on a strange water-steed inviting him into a new world. Behind her back, the air moved as if great green leaves stretched open and closed.

I'd be a fool to turn down such a chance.

"I will," he promised.

"Your vow then?"

"Yes. I vow it. Three days," he swore.

Ivy took his hand and, with surprising strength, pulled him up behind her. There were no wings blocking his view, but he felt as if they'd brushed against him. Leafy, feathery shapes, slid over his cheek as he settled on the water-made horse.

Briefly, Jack wondered what he'd done when the chiming of glass bells came again. This time like the crash of falling ice all around them. It didn't seem like a good omen.

Whatever it was, though, Jack was only there for three days. How much could go wrong in only three days?

Chapter 2: In which Jack sees the forest in an altogether new way

❦

As the horse sped past fields into the edge of the wood, Jack clung to Ivy. Creatures didn't move this fast. They didn't run so quickly that their hooves forgot to touch the ground.

Jack couldn't decide if he was excited or about to throw up. He had tried gazing at the horse's massive neck, but too soon found his vision blurring: the horse was not white at all, but jumbled hues like the inside of an abalone shell.

Finally, after what was either hours or a second, Ivy tugged the vine looped lightly around the horse's neck, stopping them as suddenly as they'd started. Glaring into the shadowed branches above them, Ivy asked, "Why are you still waiting here? I said I'd be along."

They were in a grassy clearing that Jack hadn't ever seen—and he'd explored a full two days walk from the village. He peered around, seeing only brambles and close-cropped grass. He looked up. An empty bird's nest was the only thing in the tree.

She speaks to birds?

Ivy's voice dropped even lower. "I'm quite aware of what I'm doing. You needn't be involved . . ."

Birds he couldn't see or hear.

Craning his neck, Jack stared into the branches of a tree where Ivy seemed to be looking. Leaves. Branches. Maybe a bird's nest.

Maybe someone is hidden behind the leaves.

He squinted and saw . . . absolutely nothing. "Ivy? Who are you talking to?"

"The Ellyllon . . ." Ivy glanced into the branches again, put her hands on her hips, and frowned. "*Meddlesome* Ellyllon actually, that's what they are. If they want to avoid the troubles to come, they ought to go home where it's safe." She pursed her lips. "If they had any sense whatsoever, they'd go home."

"Ellyllon?" Jack repeated, staring into the seemingly empty air.

"Tiny faeries, Jack." Ivy looked back at him.

"Where?" He spun around to try to see them.

She snorted, a silly sound he wouldn't ever have thought a faery could make, and said, "Though they claim they're big enough to defend themselves against clumsy mortals. Stop thrashing about so."

"Defend themselves? I'm no threat to them."

Ivy stared back towards the trees where the Ellyllon apparently were. "Still and true, Daisy says they refuse to show themselves."

Jack sat very still, peering at the tree, covering one eye, trying to look sideways out of an eye, blinking. It was no good: he saw nothing but branches and an old nest. "If I stay still, can I see them?"

"You mean no threat to the Ellyllon. And they might do well to remember it, mightn't they?" Ivy swung her satchel up from where she had fastened it on the long vine and rummaged around in it. "I suppose there's no reason not to give you the Sight now."

She pulled a dirty clay pot out of her satchel and opened it. Inside was a milky substance that looked a bit like garden slugs. She dipped her fingers into the stuff. "Close your eyes and hold still. I don't want to get this all over your face."

Jack closed his eyes while she spread the gooey cream on his eyelids. It burned even through the lids, so he kept his eyes closed until Ivy said, "Open up, Jack Merry, and see the world you've been blinded to."

When Jack opened his eyes, his mouth opened too. Zooming about like mad dragonflies were three tiny winged girls. Like Ivy, their eyes were almost solid black; their hair seemed normal shades of browns and blonde, albeit in deeper hues, but their skin . . . Their skin was a riot of colours--a periwinkle ankle faded into a leg of muted green which disappeared under random violet splashes.

"He's *staring*, Ivy!" A girl with violet eyes and a fierce snarl hovered beside him. She snorted, "Cattle are brighter than this one! And *they* give sweet, sweet milk. What good is he?"

The other two zipped closer, flying in darting movements, sudden and strangely rhythmic. Briefly, Jack wondered if dragonflies were all secretly faeries.

Their speech pattern grew quicker, as their sentences tumbled into each other. "The *geas*, Ivy . . ."

"We must be careful . . ."

"Foolish, that's what it is!"

Jack closed his eyes for a second, listening; then, he turned in the direction of the snarling girl. Opening his eyes, he peered directly at her face. "You are truly amazing."

All three girls stopped darting.

"Left my quill at the lake . . ." Jack stared at the Ellyllon all the while. He reached in his sack. "I have parchment. Maybe there's an extra quill . . . Do you have a quill?"

"Whatever for?"

"To sketch them." Jack turned to her. "I want to describe them. I've never thought . . . They're so beautiful."

Two of the girls alit on his shoulders. He froze.

The violet-eyed one perched on his wrist and grinned up at him. "Well, maybe he's not entirely daft . . ."

From his shoulder another Ellyll—the one with hair the colour of dandelions—muttered, "Ivy, are you sure about bringing him?"

Ivy said nothing.

The little Ellyll on his wrist grinned. "So, mortal, do you want to run while you've a chance?"

And the third—quietest—Ellyll drifted down and shushed her. "Hush, sister. The mortal has already made his choice." She peered intently at him before adding, in a tone that invited only agreement, "Haven't you?"

Jack, bemused, answered, "Why would I turn back?"

Ivy turned, then, and he saw the great feather-leaf wings he'd thought he'd glimpsed.

"This is amazing," he whispered, taking in the horse-made-of-water, the dragonfly girls, and his new leaf-winged friend. "*You're* amazing."

§

AS THEY RODE INTO THE HEART OF THE FOREST, IVY'S FEARS rose up until she felt she'd choke on them. She had considered bringing Jack Merry back home for some time, and now . . . now it was done. She'd revealed herself, given him the Sight. Once, in her childhood, a mortal would've been blinded for having the Sight, have his eyes gouged out. There was no other way to undo it. Mayhaps she should tell him. She could tell him that she needed his help, that her mother was so ill.

She glanced over her shoulder.

Jack was gazing at the Ellyllon, the horse, the wondrous-strange creatures of the wood that poked out of hidden doors and scurried away. He looked happier than she'd ever seen him in all the times she'd watched him.

Time for talking would come soon enough. "So, Jack Merry, what do think?"

He shook his head and breathed, "Amazing. It's all so amazing."

In a puddle of sunlight on the forest floor, Kayt stretched, re-positioning his long limbs in a more comfortable position. The great cat's fur grew darker: his blue-black fur absorbing the sun's rays like water seeping into soil.

He looked up and winked. "Strange indeed, this sight before me."

She nodded. "Kayt."

Kayt stretched his long pink tongue out and licked his eye. "Dare I think the talk is true? Have you brought a *mortal* among us?"

Knowing hidden others listened, Ivy raised her voice, "Jack Merry is my guest, under my protection."

"A protected guest . . ." Kayt stretched the word out like a hiss. His tail flicked, like a sinuous serpent. "What proof has he?"

Ivy pulled the silver medallion with her mark from under her tunic. Lifting the cord from around her neck, she lowered it over Jack's head. "Jack Merry bears my mark. To offer insult or harm to Jack wounds me as well."

The branches above them shimmered, revealing Cerridan—with his bark-covered limbs and leafy hair, the rowan man was hard to distinguish from the trees unless he moved.

Jack stared at him with a look of sheer awe.

Leaves brushing together in a wild symphony of forest music, Cerridan stepped to the ground and bared his mossy teeth in a smile. "Be welcome then, guest of Lady Ivy."

Jack tilted to the side, his face only a whisper away from touching those swaying leaves, and looked up at Cerridan as if to answer, but the rowan man was already ambling away, trailing music in his wake, blending into the true trees as quickly as he had unfolded from them.

Eyes wide with the wonder of it all, Jack turned to face Ivy. "I don't know why you decided to show me this, but I swear to you that I'll never forget it."

Ivy lifted her hand in caution. Her heart thudded at his foolishly chosen words. "No swearing on things, Jack. Words have power in this world."

"But I mean it. I couldn't repay you for letting me see this, not even if I spent a lifetime trying." Jack gestured at the forest, and then he lifted Ivy's medallion. "There's nothing you could ask me to do that I wouldn't at least consider. Nothing."

"Jack . . ." Ivy started. She should've talked to him, told him before she brought him home. She glanced around at the others. "He hasn't any idea what he's saying."

"Spoken and accepted." Kayt padded closer. His wide smile bared most of his teeth. "I stand witness to your vow, Mortal. May it serve the Folk."

And from the forest, myriad voices answered, "I stand witness to the vow . . ."

"And I."

"So spoken, so might it be."

❦

FROM HER PERCH IN THE TREE, CLEMATIS NUDGED DAISY. "Jack's lucky that Ivy's kind girl, unlike *some* royalty . . ."

"Clematis!" Jonquil gasped, gripping her sister's arm. "Hush now!"

She could weep for the changes that had come the past few seasons. Things weren't always like this, but speaking of it so carelessly was far from wise, especially so close to a tunnel home.

She darted over to Cerridan.

But instead of talking to her, the rowan-man leaned down from the canopy and peered at Jack. "Do you mean your vow, Jackie Mortal?" The tree man bent closer still. "Will you stand beside Lady Ivy?"

Gazing into the boughs of trees and the depths of thickets, Jonquil saw the terrified and hopeful faces waiting for Jack's answer. It had been quite a while since they had a reason for true hope. Even those above-ground would feel the ripples of change in the realm if Ivy bound herself to a mortal and challenged the queen. If a mere mortal could face the queen, what fey could do less?

Yes. Say yes.

Accepting the Queen's growing madness was folly. Suppose she willed them out of immortality? Suppose she willed them out of their very existence?

Yes, Jack Merry. Say it.

He opened his mouth.

But Ivy slapped her hand over his lips and said, "Do not answer! You don't understand!"

⁊⃛

JACK MERRY PAUSED, HIS GAZE TRAILING OVER THE CURIOUS assemblage. Tiny faces, strange and lovely, peeked out from the foliage, from hollows in fallen trees, from every shadowed spot. Others stepped into the clearing, brazen as if they were forces to be reckoned with.

And maybe they were.

Jack pulled Ivy's hand away and asked, "Did you mean it when you told me you'd be truthful with me?"

Ivy nodded.

"So, do you mean me any harm?" Jack waited, all too aware of their growing audience.

To his side was a spider of almost human proportions. It smiled. At least he hoped it was a smile that made those glittering fangs peek from her furred face.

"Will you force me to do anything?" he asked.

"No." Ivy's voice was a whisper, like a soft breeze over sheaves of wheat. She looked directly into his eyes and added, "I'll not force you to do anything."

With his new sight, Jack stared at her, seeing her features clearly now that they were face-to-face instead of astride the horse. Where the light touched her hair, the strands shimmered-- like sunlight reflecting flowers on water. Her hands, clenched tightly, were thin and her fingers longer than a human's would be.

She didn't flinch as he stared at her.

And he couldn't look away, ridiculously afraid that if he did, she'd dart into the wood as quickly as a frightened deer, leaving him with only a dream of this strange world. "I mean to stay for my three days," he said. "So tell me: what will it mean if I vow?"

She didn't move or answer.

Kayt nudged her. "Tell the mortal what he's promised, so he can answer to it."

"You haven't put a time limit on your word, Jack." Ivy paced over to a raised stone chair that Jack hadn't noticed before. Her motions were jarring, out of synch with the calmness of her voice, like she was forcing her feet to move slowly. "Supposing it were years from now, and you were an old man in your house above-ground. I could still summon you to me. You must choose the *perfect* words in vows." She raised her voice and added, "I'll not accept a vow unawares."

She caught his gaze and added in a low voice, "But others would, Jack. Some that should have honour here don't. Be careful of your words. Words are powerful here, and *vows* are laws."

Ignoring the watching crowd, Jack plopped down in front of him.

To run she'd need to kick him first, and he hoped she wouldn't do that. He glanced behind him. The Ellyllon had flown over to perch on Cerridan's branch-arms, kicking their feet and occasionally flipping backwards like the acrobats that had come through town a few seasons past. They might look relaxed, but they too watched.

Jack looked back at Ivy, speaking softly. "But I said there's nothing you could ask me to do that I wouldn't *at least consider*. I didn't say I'd dance to your every whim."

"Indeed, Jack Merry, you did add that!" Ivy gripped his shoulders in an almost-embrace. "Here I am worried after the folly of your not understanding the meaning, and you are instructing me." She stood up, still smiling, and asked, "And do you wish to make that vow still?"

And stay among them? Yes.

Jack was certain of his vow. The tiny Ellyllon, the curious cat-creature, the almost hidden creatures all waited on him to say the words, and he did. "I do."

A group of tiny hedgehog-creatures surged forward. "A blood vow, it should be a blood vow."

Ivy nodded and held out her hand, palm up.

One Hedge-Child stepped forward and bowed rather regally. Another plucked a quill from the smaller one's back and in a blur slashed open Ivy's palm. Her face was impassive as she watched bright drops of blood pool in her hand.

"Now yours, Jackie Mortal," came Cerridan's deep voice.

Jack held out his hand, wincing as the Hedge-Child drew his blood. Unlike Ivy, his face was far from impassive. Though shallow, the cut stung.

"Say it," urged Kayt, swatting Jack on the arm lightly with his tail. "Repeat the words."

Dutifully, Jack repeated, "For the three days I'm here, there's nothing you could ask me to do that I wouldn't at least *consider*."

Ivy was making a pinched face like she would speak but couldn't. She waved her hand is a "more" gesture.

So, Jack hastily added, "but consider is nor the same as do."

She let out a big gulp of air, clasped his hand in hers, and said, "Accepted!" Ivy smiled

"Heard and witnessed," answered the three Ellyllon sisters with mixed expressions on their small brows.

"Heard and witnessed," repeated Kayt, Cerridan, and many of the nameless creatures peering from around trees and shrubs.

For a moment, Jack stayed on the ground listening to the chiming of bells.

He hadn't heard them while they rode, but it occurred to him that they were connected to her somehow. Looking up at Ivy, who was still holding his hand, he asked, "Do the bells ring different ways because of how you feel? Or is it something else? Moving a certain way?"

Ivy froze, still holding his hand. "Bells?"

"I heard them earlier when I first met you, and when I agreed to stay for the three days, but I didn't hear them when we were on the horse. They're yours, aren't they?" Jack looked at her silver tunic; there were no bells to be seen. None hid in her hair that he could see.

"You hear bells?" Ivy let go of him. Her dark eyes widened. Her hands shook. He had seen that look on the faces of the townsfolk often enough in his life.

Fear.

He didn't want to see it on Ivy's face.

"Daisy!" she called out, looking around frantically.

Like a rainbow in motion, all three Ellyllon darted over.

"What's wrong?" Daisy's tiny feet touched down on Ivy's leg.

"He can hear bells," Ivy whispered, several tears slid down her cheeks. They hardened, clinking like ice as they hit the stone chair. "I wasn't sure it was even true, but he can hear the bells."

Ivy brushed away her tears with a series of clattering sounds as the last of them hit the stone in a group. "I've broken a *geas* bringing you here. If you can hear them, my lifespark is tied to your mortal span now, blown out when you pass."

"I thought faeries were immortal . . . you're going to *die* because of me?" Jack asked in horror. This wasn't what he thought he was joining on for when he took her hand at the lake. It had simply seemed like a strange adventure, too odd to turn down. He wasn't looking to get involved in something that'd cause anyone harm.

He turned to the Ellyllon. "She doesn't mean that, right?

The Ellyllon dropped their heads, not looking at him, not answering.

"Take me back," he insisted, voice lifting. "I don't want that."

"'Fey blood will be tainted by mortal ties' was the warning." Ivy took his hand in hers again. "Mother announced it. She thought it would be reason enough to stop the folk from getting involved with mortals. You're hearing my lifespark, Jack Merry. The chiming is my lifespark."

Jack let her draw him to his feet, wondering if he should let go of her hand and run. *Would she follow if I did? And what did she mean 'binding'?*

Studying her face for any sign of jest, he asked, "Why would you bring me here then? And why would your mother *not* want mortals around?"

Ivy shook her head. "You'll understand before our journey's done. " Then, her voice dropped to a whisper. "For now, know this: you are either a blessing among us or bringer of my curse. I've watched you long enough that I believe you'll not be my curse."

Chapter 3: In which Ivy's worries are answered

After they left the heart of the forest, Ivy stayed silent as they resumed their ride toward the hill. Soon they would approach the mouth of a tunnel that led to the faery realm. There was no turning back after that.

But the closer they came to the gate, the more Ivy felt her heart speeding.

Is this the mortal taint? the feeling of terror, of urgency?

She wondered if Jack's life would be long, for if her fate were truly tied to hers, she would share that lifetime, expiring when he did. Would the curse be undone? Even if she succeeded, her mother's will was still that which made the realm.

Could he change that?

Could he do it in time?

Lost in her thoughts she ignored Jack for some time, but he didn't seem to mind. He sat lightly behind her, listening instead to the Ellyllon's wild tales.

As they approached the gate, Clematis pointed out the Red-Caps on Sentry Duty, the Queen's first line of defense. Towering over most folk, they guarded their post as much by implied menace as by actual force. Thick jowled and heavily armed, they were an imposing sight.

Behind them was a dark hollow in the earth, invisible to mortals without the Sight. The air there was still, as silent as Ivy imagined a grave might be, and foreboding to even those few creatures of the wood that didn't *See*.

Home or not, Ivy's skin still tingled uncomfortably. No one crossed into that shadowed realm without the Red-Caps' leave.

Clematis whispered to Jack, "And do you know what makes their caps so red, Jack Merry?" She paused, and then, in a gleeful voice, exclaimed, "Battles! . . . a great many battles protecting us from invaders. They dip their caps in the blood of the invaders. The deeper the red, the fiercer the warrior!"

The Red-Caps, with their acute hearing, grinned. In some strange twist of reality, Clematis had become like a favorite daughter to the Red-Caps. Even the oppressive feeling at the gate didn't deter Clematis from visiting them regularly; she'd happily spend days alongside the Red-Caps, listening to their gruesome tales of battles.

Clematis darted forward—her feet brushing Ivy's wrist—and waved cheerily, and then just as suddenly went back and nudged Jack. "Be friendly."

Jack nodded, but said nothing.

Ivy sat straighter, hoping that Arth and the others were willing to let her cross. If they stopped her, she didn't know that Jack was ready to answer anything.

Would his answers satisfy them? Maybe if she stopped here, she could explain . . . explain what, though? That there was a revolution at hand? That he was her secret weapon?

"Ivy?" Jack leaned closer and murmured in her ear. "They're watching us."

"They're on duty, Jack." Ivy sighed: she should've taken time for stopping and talking. "They watch everything that passes here. Mortals come and go under their watch, and no one the wiser, but you see them, Jack. You are aware, and that changes everything."

One Red-Cap stepped forward. "Why should we let you pass?"

Ivy tugged gently on the reins; the horse stilled, as watchful as the Red-Caps. "I've been above-ground, but I'm for home now. My companions come with me."

"With a mortal?" asked one of the fiercest of the guards.

A few guards glanced over at them, but they stayed as silent as if they hadn't heard the exchange. It took a lot to distract a Red-Cap.

Ivy swallowed hard, fighting the fear that threatened to rise up. "I say he is welcome among us." She met the senior Red-Caps' gaze, and then the other strongest fighters, each in turn. "He wears my mark. He crosses with me."

"Send him forward then, Princess. Let us speak with your mortal." Arth's somber tone betrayed his worry. For all his scars and battles, he'd always been tender to her.

Ivy looked over her shoulder to face Jack. "Go on now."

He lifted one eyebrow. "Princess? I'm traveling with a faery *princess?*"

"I'm not the eldest daughter, Jack. It hardly signifies." Ivy couldn't tell him how little regard her mother had for her, to speak thus would be treason, regardless of the truth of it.

So, she squeezed his arm. "Go on now . . . the Red-Caps have called you. I cannot offer you any aid here. Just remember, be generous and speak only the truth. Always speak` truth, Jack."

❧

JACK LOOKED AT THE RED-CAPS. ONE HAD A SCAR THAT RAN the length of his cheek, disappearing under a bright red stain where his eye should be. He grinned, wrinkling that red patch of skin.

Another curled her lip in what looked like a snarl, but might have been a smile. It was hard to tell. Then that Red-Cap moved away, switching her post with another equally scarred guard.

Watching them, Jack realized that they all moved about in a complex rotation, enabling new eyes to gaze in different directions every few moments. And as they walked--despite the wicked daggers and one particularly vicious looking scythe they carried-- they were almost silent.

Gripping his sack, he slid to the ground and walked towards the Red-Caps, measuring his steps to the rhythm of his pounding heartbeat. The closer he got, the larger the strange creatures seemed.

One spread his feet in a stance better suited to wielding weapons than to making idle conversation. Another rested a hand on the hilt of a black dagger.

'Be friendly; be generous,' they said. I can do that.

"It's hot out here." Jack forced himself to hold his voice even, telling himself they were no different from the townsfolk. Maybe they were a bit scarred, but they were people just the same.

How do I greet a tired farmer? Try that.

"Can I offer you a share of my water while we talk?"

"Poisoned, is it?" one growled, giving a flash of her jagged teeth. "No mortal poison for us."

"No." Jack moved closer still. He could do this, talk to them, just like when he shared a cup of warm cider with the townsfolk. A bit of refreshment, some talk--it'd be fine. He rummaged around in his sack until he found the flask. "It's just water I had in my pack."

One of the Red-Caps stared at him.

He held it up, shaking it so it sloshed against the sides. "It's fresh, drawn from the spring this morn."

Another snorted, "You think to poison us to get by? No."

The others made agreeing noises, shuffling around, looking not at him but out through the trees even as they spoke. "Skewer him, that'd be the way."

"Peel him, I say."

Jack glanced back at Ivy. She sat astride her horse, face unreadable; the little Ellyllon hovered near her shoulder, carefully avoiding becoming entangled in Ivy's hair.

Jack turned back to the Red-Caps. Their doubts made him all the more determined to get them to share a drink with him. "If it were poison, would it make me ill?"

They conferred.

One Red-Cap From stepped from behind the others. He slid his hand over his chin; then, he grinned. "Mortals 're same as us. Poison me; poison you."

Another Red-Cap stepped around behind Jack, standing between him and Ivy. He scratched his scalp, shifting his dark red toboggan-cap in the process. His hand came away wet and red. "We could string him up for the Twitches. They like tender meats. They'd owe us."

Jack tried not to stare at the dark red fluid on the Red-Cap's fingernails: he knew what it was and wondered how recent the Red-Cap's fight had been that his cap was still wet.

Taking a deep breath, Jack returned to the question. "So, if it's safe for me, it's safe for you?"

The Red-Caps finally allowed that if Jack could drink the water it was, in fact, safe.

So, he uncorked the flask and tilted it to his mouth. He took a long swallow, careful not to waste any.

Several of the Red-Caps watched Jack while others continued their shifting and scanning the surrounding wood.

"No poison," said Jack, holding it out. "Have some, and then we can talk about what you wanted to know. I could spin a tale for you if you'd like. First, a drink between friends . . ."

"Friends, is it, now?" The Red-Cap with the stained fingernails took the water. "You offer us a vow of friendship?"

"Sure. Friends." Jack stepped back and looked up at the towering guards. Several of them were now watching him openly.

Others grinned at him. "If you don't want me to tell a tale, I'd love to hear your stories, listen to what you can tell me. I collect stories too."

With a surprisingly deep chuckle, the Red-Cap held out the flask. "Indeed?"

"I could sketch some too, not like the artists that I'm sure live here somewhere, but I'd try my best to do right by you. I'd write them down." Jack was growing excited by the idea.

Yes, I'll make a book of it, with one of those soft leather covers like the schoolmaster's fine books.

"A mortal tale-teller with the princess . . ." The Red-Cap clamped a heavy hand on Jack's shoulder. "And offering friendship to a Red-Cap?" He chuckled, shaking his head just fast enough that a few bright red drops flew from it. "Who ever heard of such a thing?"

"Well, Ivy and Clematis seemed to think you were nice . . ."

"Stop back by after your visit, if you're able, Friend. We'll trade tales with you. Go on now." He gestured for Jack to go back to the horse and bowed his head to Ivy. "He hasn't a clue, has he?"

"He knows enough for now, Arth," Ivy murmured. She held out her hand to Jack. "Come, Jack. You've done what needed doing here."

Jack looked from the Red-Cap Arth to Ivy, sure he was missing something. "I thought they needed to talk to me about something."

The Red-Caps chuckled, shaking their heads and exchanging looks.

"They did, Jack. They needed to know your intent, to test you. You've invoked a plea of friendship, meant true. They'd 've known if you'd meant it as a ploy, Jack Merry, and we'd have gone no further. But laws are what they are. You offered true friendship and bear no threat to the realm." She held out her hand. "Come now, Jack. We've a ways to travel still."

&.

"MATTY!" ARTH MOTIONED CLEMATIS CLOSER, DARTING HIS
eyes to the side, signaling her to lead them to privacy.

She grinned and snatched his crimson cap from his head. She
flew just beyond his reach, clutching his cap. "Aah, it must be
horrid to be so big and ungainly."

The Red-Caps laughed, dark husky sounds that never failed to
make Clematis feel proud that such fierce creatures welcomed
her.

Arth mock-growled. "I'm not sure why we don't squash you.
Like a little bug, Matty, that's what you are."

Stilling her wings, she let herself float downward using Arth's
cap like a sail to slow her.

He darted out a powerful hand to grab her, and she took off as
fast as she could.

As always, he followed, only a breath behind her. Without
looking, she knew the other Red-Caps were filling in the gap from
his leaving his position. *Brilliant tacticians, they were.*

When they were a little further away, Arth lowered his voice,
only the barest rasp of sound came out. "Good move, girlie."

Preening, she fluttered around so Arth could keep his back to
the others. It wasn't wise to let them see the words on Arth's lips-
-just in case. "What's the news?"

"Grandmother Nogs sent one of her boys out. Princess Ada's
voice is more and more in the royal ear." There were deep
shadows under Arth's great blue eyes. "Trouble's coming, Matty.
Word is already traveling all over the realm."

"You worry too much." She swooped forward and dropped his
cap on his head. "Queen might be mad, and Ivy might believe
herself in danger, but she's the *princess*. She'll be fine."

He pretended to swipe at Clematis. "I'm serious. You be
careful."

He lifted his hand to rub his chin, and between two fingers

was a tiny dagger, just her size. Still whispering, he said, "Grand-mother Nogs says she'd send more if she knew what to send . . . If the Queen sees Ivy's actions as a threat . . ."

"Longbow." Clematis darted over and kissed the center of the scar on his forehead. "I want a longbow. The boys showed me how to use it. I'm getting good, too."

"Clematis!" Daisy called.

"Go on." Arth shooed her like she was a bug. "Be careful, and I'll pass your word to Grandmother Nogs and any who cross." He paused. "Jack Merry might be just a mortal, but he's a good sort. Send us word if trouble comes too heavy for you."

She nodded and zipped over just as Daisy was lowering herself to Jack's shoulder.

Clematis hovered in front of Jack's face, pausing to peer at him again. He didn't look at all like she imagined a legend would look, what with his dull-colored hair and not a scar on his face. He was all legs, not thick and sturdy like the Red-Caps. She shook her head; Arth worried over nothing.

The Queen might be irritated, but once she saw that Jack Merry was just a normal mortal, it would all be fine.

Why even the lowest of the fey used to bring mortals to the realm. The Queen herself had invited mortal bards to her presence not too long ago. Yes, it'd be quite all right . . .

Or at least it would after they passed the Twitches.

Chapter 4: In which Twitches wait in every alcove

"Ivy?" Jack leaned closer to Ivy, his voice soft as he asked, "Could you tell me what's going on?"

Gazing at the shadowed grove ahead, Ivy let the horse have his head; they were close enough to home that trying to guide him was of little use. "You were brave with the Red-Caps. And kind. They'll well remember."

Jack nodded, as if he understood.

"Listen, Jack Merry." Ivy glanced back at him, keeping her voice low, and added, "There are other troubles we'll face. Mortals don't enter the realm. Mother has been very careful to set up obstacles. Heed me if I speak, strange though my suggestions might sound."

He grinned, gesturing at the Ellyllon and back towards the Red-Caps. "It all seems strange."

Ivy shook her head. He would be as helpless as a mewling babe if he didn't listen better than this. "And if I don't speak of it, Jack, heed that as well. Some things are forbidden me to tell you. Some questions are not mine to answer."

"I understand."

Ivy wondered if he'd come with her if he truly did understand;

she knew she should tell him. She'd need to tell him before they reached the Queen's presence, but how do you tell someone you're asking him to enter a fight that isn't his own? How do you say that you think they might be a weapon? Or that the queen would want to stop him if she thought Ivy was right?

". . . vicious." Clematis was still going on about the Twitches. "No sense of fun, at all. Why, when I tried to show them how to do a hurtling-dive. . ."

"Clematis, you can't blame them for being upset over that." Daisy's exasperation with Clematis' ill-thought adventures was as constant as her inevitable patience afterwards. "You were careless."

Jonquil wandered off to check on a tunnel-mouse that had crossed their path.

"Careless?" Indignant, Clematis' voice rose again. "I am a very fine diver!"

Ivy smiled, listening to the familiar arguments. The Ellyllon had often crossed the tunnel, despite having to endure the Twitches' foul temper to do so.

Jack leaned forward. "So, would the Red-Caps really have forbidden you to go home?"

"They're sworn to the Queen, Jack. They'll bleed anyone they deem a threat to the realm."

"But you're the princess!"

"Not the eldest. Being the Queen's own will save me from some dangers, but beyond that . . ." Ivy shook her head. There was much that Jack would need to learn. She shrugged, thinking of her mother's oft-repeated reminder: *Justice first, sentiment if there's time left after.* "There are no guarantees of safety. Not with the Red-Caps or anyone here."

And with that, they entered the shadows.

❧

No MATTER HOW MANY TIMES THEY CROSSED INTO THE TUNNEL, Clematis never quite got over the clammy-slick feeling down the lines of her wings. She shivered: her wings weren't made to be wet.

From her perch on Jack Merry's shoulder, she stared down the tunnel; even the glistening crystals on the walls looked ominous. Still, she watched the shifting shadows, as if seeing the Twitches' before they struck would help. It wouldn't. Nothing would.

Jonquil settled beside her. "Maybe they've fed well enough to be civil."

With a shake of her head, Clematis muttered, "Not likely."

"Shh!" Daisy tugged them down, pulling them into the slight space between Jack Merry and Ivy. "Just let Ivy speak. Don't be afraid. "

Clematis sniffed: she could speak reasonably if she had a mind to. It just so happened that the Twitches didn't give her good cause to be reasonable. She wasn't afraid, either. She only leaned closer to her sisters because of the damp. Really.

They stayed like that, tucked between Jack and Ivy like so much baggage, as they continued down the tunnel.

Then, they heard it—that rising shrill, like a banshee trapped in a box. Nothing good ever follows sounds like that.

"Vile things," Jonquil whispered, nodding her head and staring up at Jack. "You must stay strong, Jack Merry. Be steadfast."

Jack blinked at her, swallowed hard, and lowered his arm around them, as if to protect them with his mere mortal flesh.

"It'll be fine," he said, clearly, as if his heart wasn't racing.

But Clematis could see the thrum of his vein under his skin, like a bodhran drum set to life on its own accord. She patted his arm. "No. It won't."

Then the Twitches descended, talons outstretched, shrieking so loudly that Clematis' thought for sure that her ears would bleed.

❧

"Steady now, Jack Merry," Ivy shouted as she drew the braided reins through her hand. "They're not as frightening as they appear."

"Really?" Jack looked at the creatures hurtling towards them with their mouths wide open. Their bodies were as thin as bare bones, covered in rotting grey skin that fluttered with a wet smacking sound. Sprouting from their sickly skin were wings, as long as their bodies but far sturdier. "They look awfully angry."

"They'll bluster a bit, but they're not usually more than an irritation." Then, Ivy frowned.

The creatures were still coming towards them, only now their talons were outstretched.

Ivy bent forward and spoke something over the braid.

As Jack watched, the braid hardened into a lengthy staff which Ivy promptly raised and wielded against the oncoming Twitches.

The Twitches' mouths yawned open, wider than should be possible, baring toothless gums as they shrieked, "Noooooo . . ."

Their objection echoed through the damp tunnel, *no-no-no-no*, deeper in reverberation than their shrill screams.

Jack ducked, twisting away from outstretched talons, keeping the little Ellyllon close to his chest as he moved. "Suggestions, Ivy?"

"Patience. They're trying to frighten us." She deflected the assault of another set of talons. "They'll settle soon enough if we've the patience."

Jack glanced down at the Ellyllon. "Are they always like this?"

"Told you they were nasty," Clematis said in a wavering voice. "But they're usually just bothersome and noisy, no sense of style or manners."

"Are you trying to get eaten?" Daisy tugged Clematis closer and clamped a hand firmly over her mouth. "Shush!"

Jack shook his head at the girl's audacity. He looked around at the Twitches, swirling and swooping to avoid Ivy's rope-that-was-now-a-weapon. "They look strong."

"Clever too, but your flattery won't work on these ones." Ivy thwacked a Twitches' leathery wing with a thick sound. "Come now! I've as much right to cross as I did this morning."

"Queen's orders, Princess Ivy," shrilled one Twitch.

The others promptly took up the words, "Queen's orders . . ."

"So, say the Queen, and so we do."

Clematis muttered, "Because they don't have the sense to . . mgfl."

Daisy clamped her hand over Clematis's mouth to cut off her undoubtedly hostile retort.

Glancing down, Jack winked at Clematis who was struggling against her sister's firm grip.

Just then Daisy shrieked, yanking her hand away from Clematis' mouth abruptly.

"You bit me!" Daisy's wings whirred as she fluttered into the air. "I can't believe you bit me."

Clematis grabbed Daisy's ankle and yanked her back, screaming, "Ivy! The other side . . ."

As Jack watched, a hideous Twitch barreled towards them with startling speed, staring at the Ellyllon like a predator homing in on wounded prey. Its eyes glowed like some alchemists' unearthly brew.

Ivy wouldn't be fast enough this time.

He lifted his arm, using it to block the opening between his body and Ivy's back. The Twitches' talons pierced his skin, tearing a slash from his wrist to elbow.

Ivy bashed it on the head, beating it backwards ferociously.

Clematis let out a howl. "Vile, retched things! Do you hear me?!"

Dark droplets poured from his arm, dripping on the little Ellyllon as they struggled to keep Clematis calm.

Looking like a small warrior with her fierce snarl, she yelled,

"Ivy ought to banish the bunch of you. An infestation, that's what you are!"

"I can't believe they're attacking me." Ivy beat back another Twitch. "They've never done that."

But it went on like that until Jack was near numb to the sight; his arm ached something awful. He cradled the Ellyllon in his other arm, watching the Twitches carefully lest one of them got past Ivy.

The tunnel echoed with the Twitches' shrilling, and the steady thumps as Ivy flailed against the seemingly endless onslaught of Twitches.

As far as Ivy could see, Twitches eyes glowed from the shadows. Though they had finally settled, retreating to their roosts, she feared it was but a temporary calm.

Her stomach was quavering, and her arms throbbed. She bit down on her lip and looked over the others. Jack had more than a few scratches and that one deep gash on his forearm. The bone wasn't showing, but it didn't look good all the same. Jonquil and Daisy were so busy keeping Clematis still and silent that they hadn't had time to wipe away Jack's blood from where it'd dripped onto them.

"Sorry, Jack," she murmured. "The Twitches aren't usually so . . . dangerous."

He nodded, gravely. Then, he said, to no one and everyone, "So, what can we do about this difference of opinion?"

Ivy's hand clenched around the still-solid braid, not at all certain if the Twitches would attack again or not.

From the darkness, they called, "Bringing the human here . . . in our den."

"Queen said no. She did."

"It needn't be this way." Ivy tried to stop them before they got spun up again. "I am the Queen's own. This is my right, my home."

No one spoke, the tunnel's silence broken only by the dripping of water into stagnant pools and the scraping of talons on rocks as the Twitches shifted and squirmed.

Glad the horse's hooves were soundless, Ivy urged him slowly forward.

She tried not to stare at the eyes glowing in the darkest of the shadows. *Steady,* she told herself. *We'll get through this.*

"Who risks the Queen's ire?" The Twitches started off again, repeating the word like a battle cry, *ire-ire-ire,* and swooping through the air.

Ivy straightened her spine, watching those glowing eyes advancing on them again.

Vaguely, she heard Jack mutter, "Sorry" as he swung his satchel around the front of his body and tucked the Ellyllon into it. "You're safer in there."

But once they were overhead, the Twitches just circled.

"I'm not sure I'm up for much more of this." Ivy wiped her hair from her eyes and stared at the Twitches, trying to keep alert. She whispered a plea that she was right and said, "Tell me a story, Jack Merry."

"A story?" Jack repeated. "Perhaps now's not the best time."

A particularly raucous cry sounded down the tunnel, and the Twitches stopped circling and pulled back against the walls.

"No, Jack Merry, now is the perfect time. Close your eyes and tell me a story in which the heroes defeat their foes." Ivy urged the horse to go a bit faster and pleaded, hoping she was right, "Tell me a tale that I can believe with my every breath, Jack."

Another flock of Twitches flew toward them, each clutching something large and dark in her talons. As the flock came closer, the air became thick with a foul odor.

"Now, Jack!"

The flock of Twitches began dropping putrid egg sacks in

their path. Viscous brown fluid oozed from them, sliding down the cave walls where they hit with loud thuds, clogging the ground where they spilled and shattered.

If they weren't through the tunnel soon, the horse's hooves would be stuck in the vile stuff, just as their feet would be if they were to try to walk through it.

It splattered on them, and Ivy leaned forward and tangled a hand in the horse's mane, hoping that she'd be able to get free without too much pain once they were through the tunnel. She tightened her legs around the horse. "Close your eyes and tell me the story, Jack."

§

AND SO, JACK BEGAN TO TELL A TALE. "THERE ONCE WAS A foolish mortal boy who stumbled into an incredible world . . ."

Ivy interrupted, "When they met dangerous enemies, Jack, that's where the story is now . . . they were against uncommon awful odds, and what happened, Jack Merry? How did the next thing come to pass?"

"Right, then, they were facing awful enemies, coming at them from every side . . ." Jack paused, opening his eyes to look around. They really *were* coming at them from every side. His mouth was dry.

"Queen says the human shall not pass." The Twitches dropped their fetid sacks, spreading that gummy gunk in the horse's path. "Keep you here, says the Queen."

"Jack! Close your eyes and tell." Ivy's voice was louder this time. "Trust me. Remember? You said you'd trust me."

Right, thought Jack. "So, the heroes were under assault, and the girl, though she was braver, was growing tired. Suddenly, though, she realized they were almost past their enemies. Yes, they were going to be safe. She felt stronger, her arms no longer tired from their fierce battles. She lifted her sword . . ." He faltered, almost believing he really had heard the whistle of a sword swinging through the air.

One of the Twitches shrieked.

In a strange voice, Ivy urged, "Keep going, Jack. 'She lifted her sword,' and then what?"

A Twitch swooped close enough that Jack felt its breath on his face. It crooned in that horrendous voice, "In the tunnel you must stay. We'll feast on your soft flesh."

Jack shivered. "And she had the strength of . . ."

Another Twitch swooped lower, moaning, "Mortal and princess too . . ."

Another whistling sound, not a thwack, came from in front of him. Something thick and warm splashed on his face, burning where it hit, like hot tallow.

"I want their eyes," shrilled a Twitch above them. "Tasty, like sweetmeat . . ."

He felt Ivy's back stiffen and then the feel of her hair as she leaned back, forcing him to bend too. "Of what, Jack?" she prodded. "Tell me how strong she was."

Droplets and thicker things fell on Jack's arm.

Eyes firmly closed, Jack kept telling, "She had the strength of a score of Red-Caps. She was a blur, a fierce and strong princess swinging her unbreakable sword, cutting through the foes with as much ease as if she were walking through the forest, and then . . ."

"And could their foes keep up with her?" Ivy interrupted again. "Picture them, Jack. Picture their foes, and tell me of them."

Jack shook his head. "No, she looked at them and realized they weren't as clever or fast as they thought they were." He paused, picturing their own foes as clearly as if his eyes were open: imagining the Twitches careening into the damp caves walls, hideous wings failing them. "They were exhausted, unable to face the princess' ferocious attack, and they grew clumsy and tired."

He turned his head towards a strange series of thuds and shrilling cries.

"Keep your eyes closed, Jack Merry." Ivy exclaimed. "I need your *words*. Tell me what came next. When she looked, how close was the end of the tunnel?"

Jack felt dizzy and for a moment feared he'd fall. "Oh, they were almost out. It was only another moment, and then they were safe . . ."

"We're here, Jack Merry." Ivy sounded strange, like she was near to laughing or crying or maybe both. "We're here, and we're quite all right."

As he opened his eyes, Jack heard the bells, but they rang loudly like heavy silver now, not at all like fragile glass now.

Chapter 5: In which they come to a meadow where a meadow shouldn't be

As Jack looked around, he had the illusion that they were in a meadow lit by the midday sun--until he looked up into the sky where stalactites hung from the cave-like ceiling.

On the ground, moss-covered rocks broke through the thick ferns. Strange birds flittered around, with eyes big as the bottoms of mugs. In front of them, a pond of orange water rippled as if a strong breeze played over the surface. It was stunning.

But Jack was too tired to want to explore.

Odd, he thought, *considering that all I did was sit there while Ivy fought off the Twitches.*

Dizzy, he slipped from the back of the horse and settled on a mossy rock. Gently, he opened his sack and peered inside. "Come on, now. We're past the Twitches."

The Ellyllon crept out, strangely silent. Even Clematis seemed subdued.

"We are indebted to you, Jack Merry," Jonquil murmured before buzzing off in the direction of a vibrant squirrel with an extra tail or two.

Jack realized he was sitting down--gaping at their surroundings--when it was Ivy that had done the hardest work. He struggled to stand. "Do you need help?"

"No, Jack Merry. Sit and rest. I'll not ask more of you just now, not after all you've done." Ivy unwound her fingers from the horse's mane--wincing as her skin tore and bled--and slid down to stand beside him. She nodded to the horse. "Go on."

The horse bowed its head and galloped toward the orange pond, beginning to melt before it even reached the water.

Jack watched the horse sink into the water, leaving no trace of its presence behind. "I was useless, no weapon. I did nothing but prattle on while you . . ."

"Hush. You've done far more than you realize . . . and you've shed blood for the Ellyllon, Jack. There's great honor in what you did." Ivy handed him an iridescent cloth. "You could have avoided that blow if you let the Twitches near the Ellyllon."

Jack tried to wipe the sticky brown goop from his face and neck, considering. He'd been an outcast his whole life--tolerated, sure, but truly accepted . . . not ever. He'd spent years dreaming that one day he'd find that the stories were true, that one day he'd be whisked away into a world where he mattered.

Shaking his head, he said, "No. I couldn't have."

Perhaps, later there'd be time enough to think about what would come. For now, he needed to get rid of the brown sludge on his skin and rest a while. He gestured toward the pond. "Can I wash in that water?"

IVY NODDED, LETTING OUT THE BREATH SHE'D BEEN HOLDING while Jack was thinking. He wasn't asking any questions, didn't seem even to think of asking about their narrow escape from the Twitches. She needed to tell him. She'd suspected that he could do it, could bend the world, but to see the truth of Jack's gift . . . well, it was a marvelous thing indeed.

As she watched, her horse re-formed just enough to spit streams of orange water at the Ellyllon.

Still unsteady on his feet, Jack settled at the water's edge with the Ellyllon.

As the horse continued to surface and dowse them, Jonquil darted towards the shore. Legs dripping, she plopped down on a toadstool.

Daisy dried her face with a large violet, before announcing, "I'm going to forage for something to eat."

Jack dipped Ivy's iridescent cloth in the water, wrung it out, and held it out to Jonquil. In the process, the severity of the wound on his arm was exposed to her for the first time.

With a gasp, Jonquil darted off, returning promptly with a length of spider's lace and a bundle of moss.

"Stay still." She positioned a section of moss over Jack's bleeding arm and began weaving the spider's lace over it to tether the moss to the wound, muttering, "We can't be having him sick. Indeed. Injured so soon . . . too much to do."

All the while, Clematis sat rather silently on Jack's shoulder, watching her sister work. After Jonquil was done, Clematis still stared at Jack's arm. "Perhaps it'd been wiser to leave Jack at the lake."

Feigning patience, Ivy walked over and sat down on a damp rock beside Jack. "Wiser today, perhaps, but things don't get better for delaying what needs done."

Clematis folded her arms over her chest. "He doesn't even know what he can do."

"*I* didn't know before, not for certain." Ivy thought of all the times she'd thought about doing this, risking it, but her courage had failed her every time—until today. "If I'd fetched him last harvest, or even last moon, how different would it'd have been?"

"Fetch me?" His voice was woozy now.

The combined force of blood loss and using his gift for the first time had worn him out at last.

Easing closer to Jack in case he toppled, Ivy glanced at Clematis. The temperamental Ellyll's wings fluttered so forcefully that she floated slightly above Jack's shoulder.

Ivy took a handful of moss and began using it as a sponge, dipping it in the water and trying to wash away the brown sludge and other things that clung to her skin.

Finally, Clematis slumped onto Jack's shoulder, petting his ear in a brief show of affection. "I just don't like it. Don't like what happened in the tunnel; don't like would could happen if the Queen realizes the legends were true."

"I'm scared, too." Ivy tried to keep her voice steady. Letting them hear how very terrified she was wouldn't do a moment's good. "But the alternatives all failed. I hoped she'd get well, but I *can't* just let things go on this way. The realm remakes itself in the Queen's image, and unless the Queen is well . . ."

Jonquil darted over, murmuring to Clematis, tugging her away. "Come now. It'll all be quite fine."

But Clematis had never been one to take well to tender emotions. She yanked her arm free from her sister's grasp and fled behind a clutch of wildflowers.

"You're doing the right thing, Ivy." Jonquil smiled briefly before darting after Clematis, calling back, "Remember that."

"Fetch me?" Jack mumbled.

"Shush, now, Jack Merry." Ivy helped him lean back. The morrow was soon enough for talking. "Talk will come later. Take a rest. You've earned it."

❦

JONQUIL SNAGGED A WING ON A BROKEN TWIG HIDDEN IN THE thick plant-cover. Sometimes she was certain Clematis didn't have an easy emotion in her entire being. Far less painful to apply salve to a wounded Hedge-Child than sooth Clematis. The Hedge-Children squirmed, but at least they appreciated the salve.

Clematis looked up as Jonquil touched down beside her. "We could've all died in there."

Jonquil nodded—and waited.

She wished she could tell her about the plans she'd made, the shadowed meetings she kept secret so long, but Clematis wasn't looking for answers, not yet. After, well, then she'd be ready to listen, but she needed to talk first.

"I mean the Twitches aren't ever *pleasant*. Still and all, I figured Ivy's visits to the mortal town were just a game, figured the legends were a grand lie, nothing serious enough to endanger the Queen." Clematis tugged at little tufts of moss, absently, not hard enough to rip them free of the rocks. "I didn't know he mattered. Just a mortal that caught Ivy's attention . . ."

"Things have been getting steadily worse." Jonquil kept her voice low and melodic. "If you knew, would you have tried to stop her?"

Clematis frowned. "Well, no, but he's here, and he does change things. Once the Queen hears, we're truly in danger."

From above them Daisy's voice joined in, "If you'd have known, you'd have helped her."

She dropped down to stand in front of them, hands on her hips, looking more like their mother every moment. "You've been vocal enough about the changes in the realm to end up in the Queen's ill graces a number of times. If the Queen were to start taking your belligerence seriously . . ." Frowning, she tapped her foot on the hard ground.

There is no peace being the middle sister, Jonquil thought yet again. Maybe that's why she'd ended up mediating in so many meetings. *Even the feral folk are more amenable than Matty and Daisy most days.*

She stifled a sigh and glanced at Clematis, whose violet eyes glowed angrily. "Clematis has never feared trouble."

Almost casually, Clematis tugged a flower down by the stem and rubbed her cheek on the white petals. "Perhaps you could go stay with Uncle Connlin for a while. Harvest isn't truly that far away, and he could use the help."

"No. I've waited for this to come to pass." Jonquil smiled to soften her tone. "I'll stand with Ivy and Jack. One of them's as likely as not to be injured, and neither knows a thing about healing. And you?"

Daisy shrugged. "There's nowhere except above-ground that's going to be truly safe now, not until this is done, and hiding up there is not for me."

"And if Ivy fails? What if one of you get hurt or worse?" Clematis kept her face hidden in the flower, but the rising tone in her voice betrayed her anger. "What then?"

"We won't." Jonquil cupped her sister's face and forced her to look at them. She smoothed her sister's hair back and whispered, "You'll have your own battle-tales to tell Arth, afterwards."

"I heard that," Daisy muttered, but she picked up the thread and kept on, distracting her sister. "If I'd have known that lolly-gagging with the Red-Caps would encourage you so . . . well, I'd have done something about it."

Straightening her back, Clematis said, "Arth said he'd talked to the Bollynoggins about a longbow. Grandmother Nogs even sent me this." She pulled out a short dagger from under her tunic.

"What are you thinking?" Daisy scowled, running her hands over her face like Mother used to do when she was altogether frustrated. "You do realize that we're *tiny fey*? You're as bad as Hagan."

Leaving them to their bickering, Jonquil took to the air in search of a resting place. Her sisters would be fine. They would all be fine.

Eventually. Maybe even soon.

AS EVENING FELL, THE FALSE LIGHT FADED TO AN ARTIFICIAL

dusk. It was never truly dark in the meadow, and for the first time Ivy was glad of it.

When she was above-ground, she'd watched the stars come out, marveled at tiny points of light glimmering in the sky--like Will o' the Wisps tempting one to touch the impossible, whispering of secrets just beyond her grasp. She'd spent hours imaging the possibilities. Tonight, though, she took comfort in the starless ceiling above her; there was comfort in knowing there were no hidden reaches above her.

Listening to Jack's rhythmic breathing as he slept, Ivy walked back to the high grass where she'd dropped the sword Jack had spoken into being during their battle.

The make of it was as fine as any that the Queen's warriors carried. The blade was of forged steel, an awful thing for one of faery blood to even touch, but the guard was of silver, protecting her hand from touching that poisonous metal.

As she wiped it clean, she could see that it was, in truth, a thing a beauty: inlayed on the blade were etched vines, like those she'd braided as she sat beside Jack at the lake.

Once it was clean, she spread a cloth over the blade, hiding it from sight, and lay down beside it. But before she drifted to sleep, she slipped her hand under the cloth and rested her fingers on the hilt.

Chapter 6: In which Jack learns the truth

A foot prodded Ivy in the ribs, ribs that were already sore from yesterday's battle. Eyes closed, Ivy wrapped her fingers around the hilt of her sword, just in case. But when she opened her eyes, what she saw was worse than even the most troublesome folk. Standing in the meadow, in full court regalia, was her eldest sister, Princess Ada.

Ada kicked Ivy again, with more force this time.

Ivy sat up, but her hand was still hidden. "Ada, how very . . . surprising to see you."

Ada walked over to a massive boulder, where she could sit without soiling her robes. Her delicate sandals were already ruined, stained by the damp meadow grass, but Ada never went anywhere looking less than stunning. "You missed the dinner, Ivy. I though it prudent to see where you were."

"You were worried?" Ivy glanced at Jack, still sleeping peacefully. She wondered if it were better to let him rest or to wake him.

Ada laughed, not a real laugh, a titter. "No, dearie, I was irritated."

Ivy decided to let Jack sleep, no sense in both of them having to listen to Ada's twisted truths. Cupping her hands, Ivy scooped up water and washed her face.

For a blissful moment, Ada remained silent, but it didn't last. "Mother expected you to be there, Ivy, as did I."

"Mother doesn't even attend most of the dinners." Ivy let her hair fall forward and dipped it in the pond. She'd washed it several times last eve, but she could still smell the lingering stench of the Twitches. "Are you claiming she missed me?"

"Not really." Ada brushed a stray bit of pollen from her gown, scowling. "Yet I am curious as to why you are out here sleeping on the ground."

"We had a bit of . . . difficulty. The Twitches seemed to think I was not welcome home." Ivy glanced at Jack; his eyes were still closed. She kept her voice low. "I'm lucky to be unharmed."

Ada stood over Jack, peering down at him. She didn't touch him. "You've brought the mortal. This is the one you've watched, isn't it?"

"He wears my mark, Ada. He comes here under my protection." Ivy kept her voice calm and hoped that Ada would be polite at least.

She wasn't.

"And does that give you leave to break the Queen's *geas*? You'd anger the Queen over a foolish legend? I won't allow this." Ada stood and stepped so close that her skirts brushed Ivy's feet.

Refusing to be cowed, Ivy pushed her away. "That's not your concern, Ada. You do not wear the crown."

"But I do handle many of Mother's affairs now. She listens to me, and you'd do well to remember it." Ada's eyes narrowed. "Take the mortal back above-ground, Lillian, and leave him there. I'd loath having to tell Mother. Imagine: punished for belief in a nursery tale. You're as mad as Mother."

Ivy drew several calming breaths. She'd not show her sister the strength she'd gained by Jack's tale-telling in the tunnel, not yet.

Ada moved closer, her breath warm on Ivy's face. Smiling, she murmured, "Be a good girl, and do as I say."

It took all of her self-control to resist walloping Ada. But Ivy stepped back, fists curled, and merely watched her sister stroll away.

❦

JACK STAYED STILL, LISTENING TO IVY AND HER SISTER. MAYBE he was better off not having had a family of his own; Ivy's family seemed a lot less than pleasant. When he heard the soft sounds of Ivy sitting down beside him, Jack rolled over, wincing as he bumped his wounded arm.

"Are you awake?" Her voice wasn't much louder than the whirring of the Ellyllon's wings. "She's gone."

Surreptitiously, he glanced at Ivy's face and was relieved to see that she looked angry, not upset. He wasn't eager to repeat the whole tears bit, Ivy's crying made him decidedly uncomfortable, like he should find a way to fix *something*, and soon. "She's a real charmer."

"And that was her good mood." Ivy flashed a brief grin, before looking off into the direction Ada must have gone. Then she turned back to Jack. "Hungry?"

His initial response faded as he thought about his sack. "I don't have much left to eat."

Eyes twinkling, Ivy hopped to her feet. "Wash up, Jack Merry. We'll find you something to feast upon."

As Jack kneeled and scooped up a handful of water, he tried not to disturb the tiny fish darting in the pond. When he sat back, the fish clustered, watching him with an almost human awareness. As he leaned closer to the water, they swarmed away. Finally, they all fled to the center of the pond.

"Are you well, Jack Merry?"

He glanced up to see Jonquil, sitting on a floating leaf. Her feet were dangling in the water and the swarms of fish were poking their scaled heads out of the pond for her to pet them.

"I am. You were very gentle." He touched his bandage, realizing he'd not thanked her. "I appreciate it."

She nodded, absently, her attention still on the fish. "A word of advice, Jack Merry, in our land we don't offer thanks. It's bad manners to do so."

"Oh." He wracked his memory to think of another way to say he was thankful without saying it, and in the moment came up empty. "Can I ask what I'm to do then?"

Jonquil floated up, like a leaf lifted by the breeze. "When one does a kindness for you, remember it, and repay it as best you can. Words are powerful. Choose ones with depth."

Jack started, fearing that she thought he didn't really appreciate her gentle stitching. "But they do have depth . . ."

"No," she corrected in a voice far more melodic than her sisters'. "You know finer words than that. In this realm, choose your deeds and words with care." She hovered over the pond, dropping down to trail her toes over the surface every so often. Fish jumped up, nipping at her toes as she went.

"They *are* fine stitches, sister." With only the briefest of sounds, Clematis dropped down to stand on Jack's wrist. She leaned close to Jack's bandage. "I don't believe the White Widow herself could make finer. If it were my wound, I'd gift you with the softest fur shorn of the brightest squirrel I could find."

Jack lifted his arm so Clematis was near his face.

Lips pursed, she stared pointedly at the bandage.

"Right," Jack started. "Well, I have no idea how to convince a squirrel to share its fur, but if I could I'd give you the finest gift I could find . . ."

"Close your eyes, Jack," Clematis urged. "What do you see there that would be fit to show Jonquil the worth of her kindness?"

Why does everyone think I need to close my eyes to imagine things?

Shaking his head, Jack did as he was told and closed his eyes. He heard Ivy humming as she returned, but he kept his eyes closed, imagining what Jonquil would most appreciate. "If I could, I'd give you something precious, that no one could use but you."

"And what would that be . . ." Ivy's hand brushed his arm. "What would you offer our little healer, Jack Merry?"

At Ivy's comment, Jack felt foolish, but he'd already begun so there was no sense in backing away. "I'd offer you the gift of healing without anything but your touch."

Jack felt Clematis lift off his wrist.

"If I could," Jack lowered his voice, worried that he'd offended Jonquil.

No one spoke.

Then, Clematis' voice whispered in his ear, "Can you truly imagine that? Imagine Jonquil brushing her hand over a wound and it vanishing as if it had never been."

He nodded, picturing Jonquil as clearly as if his eyes were open.

A wave of exhaustion rolled over him, making him glad he was still kneeling on the ground. Perhaps he'd feel better after eating.

He opened his eyes to find all three Ellyllon and Ivy staring at him as if he were the oddity among them, and he supposed in some way he was. Everything here was so different that his idea of a gift was probably altogether wrong.

Then, Jonquil alit on his arm. She rested her tiny hands on his bandage for a moment and then gently slid them around the outside of the wrapping. "There would not be a finer gift you could give me."

He blinked, dizzy again. He turned to Ivy. "Perhaps we could eat. I think I'm still out of sorts from everything."

Ivy nodded and helped him to his feet. "After that, we must talk." A curious look on her face, she added, "Please, try not to judge me too harshly."

❦

As she led Jack back to the clearing where she'd left the food she'd gathered, Ivy didn't know whether to be angry with Clematis or not. She'd gone along with it, but it felt like trickery, felt wring to have Jack use his gift without meaning too. Of course, Jonquil's having the gift of healing would be a true blessing as they went on, but Jack was already exhausted.

Have we stolen her gift from him? What of his own needs?

Still and true, as she'd watched Jonquil's casual touch, Ivy was certain the Ellyll had healed Jack's arm.

"Here you are, Jack Merry." She gently helped Jack sit down on the close-cropped meadow grass. "Your first feast of faery fruits."

As he gazed at it, silent and still, Ivy feared it was less than impressive to him. There were slices of sweetroot, several whole green-birch fruit, a few winter plums, a variety of nuts, and even berries. "It was all I could find so quickly."

"No, it's great." He picked up a green-birch fruit. "I'm just not sure if I peel it or what . . ." "Just bite it." She lifted one and demonstrated.

Then, Daisy arrived, herding three scoopbacked tortoises forward, each with a crock of Drizzle Soup on its back. "Drink up. It's full of restorative plant juices."

Clematis and Jonquil exchanged a grimace.

Dutifully, Ivy lifted a crock and took a sip; it was as awful as always.

Jack lifted a hand, and she quickly put a slice of sweetroot in it. "Try this."

He ate it, and then reached out again.

"Here!" Clematis zipped up and plopped a berry in his mouth.

Covering her laugh with a cough, Ivy tried not to look at Daisy who was once again scowling.

After swallowing his berry, Jack said, "The soup smells good."

Then, to everyone's confusion he lifted the crock and drank the whole thing. "Delicious!"

Daisy preened. "Well, it's nice that *someone* here has sense."

❧

AFTER THEY FINISHED THEIR MEAL, EVEN THE DRIZZLE SOUP, Ivy turned to Jack. "I need to show you something."

Before he could answer, the Ellyllon lifted up in a whir of color. Ivy looked away, as Clematis and Jonquil both paused to pat his face with their small hands.

"Go on, now." Daisy chased them away, muttering something as she went.

"In the realm, there is a legend of mortals who can tell tales so true that they *become*." Ivy pulled a sword out from under a length of dull cloth and placed it in the grass in front of Jack. "I suppose all creatures have legends, but this legend so frightened the Queen that she forbade mortals from entering her land. Most folk see no reason to take it seriously, thinking Mother's belief foolish." She glanced at him, dark eyes wide, and added, "But even the mad have moments of insight."

Jack looked at her, and all of townsfolk's murmured fears of faeries made sense: She has deceived him. He was violating the commands of the faery queen, and Ivy knew it, encouraged it even. "Strife" she'd said, but this was not simple strife. This was treason, and he was right in the thick of it.

Seeming oblivious to his upset, Ivy ran her finger over the face of the blade where delicate blossoms were etched into the metal. "The Queen alone has power to remake the world. Her visions, her images are reality here, but she's not well." Ivy's finger began to redden and bleed. Bright red drops fell onto the sword. She held it up. "Cold steel, it's awful."

"Where did the sword come from?" he asked, although he knew. In that terrible certainty before a fall, he knew.

"Once it was a vine, and you saw me braid it." She curled her hand around the hilt. "Then it was a staff, for *my* gift will not fashion that which would carry dark intent. The Queen's will hath made it so."

With her free hand, Ivy gripped his hand and pulled it to rest on the hilt of the sword. "But your gift does not have such limits. You can change the world, Jack Merry. You can make things as they ought to be." She stared at him, and in a voice so soft it sounded like a prayer, she added, "You can heal the Queen."

"Are the Twitches injured?" Thinking about the brown stuff he'd scrubbed off his arms, Jack yanked his hand away from her. For a moment, he thought he was going to be sick. His stomach squirmed. His heart thudded. He whispered, "They are, aren't they? Why? Why would you do this?"

He got to his feet, staring at Ivy. "What happened to being truthful?"

"I vowed to do my best by you, to give you full truth by the third day. I've done that and more. If you knew what I risked for you, for this." She gestured around her, and her eyes darkened. "I'm not a vow-breaker, Jack Merry."

Jack had never been quite as furious in his life. Here he was, thinking he finally found a place where he'd be accepted, and everything was a lie. He wasn't even welcome here. Mortals were forbidden, and despite rumors and whispers, Jack Merry was completely mortal.

"This whole thing has been what? A bid for the throne? You're the youngest so you don't have any other way to get to be Queen? Is that it?"

"Haven't you been listening? My mother is ill." Ivy didn't stand. She looked up at him, her face suddenly looking far older than she seemed. "She has no control over her visions, and my sister encourages her delusions. I didn't know what else to do."

He felt himself shaking, and wasn't sure if he was more angry or hurt. "So, you tricked me? That was your plan? Trick me and get a steel sword?"

Ivy looked away, seeming to watch something beyond him. "I hoped she'd get well, but she hasn't. She grows worse. The folk meet and plot against her . . ." She caught his hand in hers, holding it with a strength far greater than seemed possible with those thin fingers. "I've watched you for many mortal years, Jack Merry. You've a good heart, and when I heard you tell your stories to the mortals there, I knew. I knew you were the sort of mortal that could *change* things."

Jack yanked his hand from her grip and walked away. He wasn't sure where he was going, but being with Ivy suddenly felt like the last place he wanted to be.

Chapter 7: In which questions must be answered

❧❀☙

Daisy watched Jack go. *He was right*, she supposed, *to think Ivy'd tricked him*. She had brought him under the earth without much warning. Mortals seldom took well to that.

"Are you going to follow him?" Daisy dropped down to peer at the sword, careful not to touch it.

"And say what?" Ivy closed her eyes, tilting her head down so her hair fell over her face like a veil. "Shall I say I'll take him above-ground? Tell him it's altogether fine if the realm falls deeper into madness?"

"Perhaps." Daisy watched her, the girl she'd tended since she was a toddling babe. She'd had far too much burden put on her so young. "It's not fine, dear, but it's not his battle."

"Mother's not going to get well without help. If we take Jack there, maybe we can talk, and even if not, maybe *he* can talk—tell a tale about her being well—and then she'd be well." Ivy's voice rose, anger or panic creeping in again. "It's worse this season, worse *every* season."

"It is." Daisy busied herself gathering up the few pieces of food not eaten and wrapping them in leaves. "But how would Jack Merry know such a thing?"

"He thinks I was untrue."

"And were you, by mortal standards?" Daisy had almost finished wrapping the food and was beginning to drag it over to Ivy's satchel. Someone had to look after the lot of them, else they'd be half-starved before they even got to see the Queen. "Truth here isn't quite the same as truth above-ground."

"I told no untruths," Ivy started in a petulant tone. "I just—"

Daisy put her hands on her hips, and Ivy stopped mid-statement.

Daisy said gently, "You've withheld the full of it."

"I hoped once he saw the realm, once he knew her, he'd understand." Ivy clenched her hands together.

But Daisy shook her head. She flew up to Ivy's shoulder and tugged a handful of hair. Smiling to soften the blow, she said, "You put off telling him, and in his world that, too, is a kind of lie. Once it was also thus in the realm."

At first, Ivy said nothing, just stared as if she were a lost child. Finally, she ducked her head. "I should talk to him."

Daisy nodded. "It would be the right thing to do."

After Ivy walked away, Daisy sat down and pulled her knees to her chest. It would be a glorious thing if they were to get through the troubles unharmed, simply walk up to the mad queen and fix things, but she doubted any of them truly understood the feat they'd undertaken.

She lowered her head, resting it on her knee. As tears slid down her cheeks and dripped onto her lap, she whispered a plea that the others wouldn't realize how little chance they had of success, that foolish belief was one of the few things they had on their side. Three Ellyllon, a mortal, and a faery . . . their odds weren't good at all.

❧

NOT FAR AWAY, JACK WALKED AIMLESSLY—UTTERLY LOST BUT

thinking he'd find the mouth of the tunnel any moment. *If the Twitches are injured or gone, why not simply walk back that way?* Of course, he wasn't entirely sure that he wanted to go, but he was certain that he couldn't just sit around waiting for Ivy to decide for him.

He nodded to himself.

Yes, indeed, this being passive is just not doing it.

He thought about the questions he might have asked, had he been a little less angry. Then he thought of the utter mess she'd pulled him into. He hadn't done much deciding at all so far, just following along without any questions. *That* needed to stop. There was no reason to stay here while he sorted it out. Why, now that he knew the way, he could come back—if he chose to, that is.

"Fancy that, a mortal that's not above-ground." A massive black dog with eyes as red as holly berries stood in front of him, blocking the way by its sheer size.

Jack tried for a friendly voice. "Would you know which way to turn if I wanted to go above-ground?"

The dog laughed; at least Jack thought it was a laugh, though it sounded deep enough that it might have been a growl. "Knowing and saying's not quite the same, is it?"

Jack sighed, entirely too tired of word games to try to reason with a dog. *Reason with a dog?* He shook his head and tried to step around the beast.

It made another sound, and this time Jack was certain it was, in fact, a growl.

Bits of spittle sprayed from its jaws. "Do you want to run?"

"Walking's fine." Jack backed away, not sure what else to do. He thought about what Ivy'd just said about his being able to speak things into being. Right now, that sounded like a good skill to have.

"Run." It growled. "I could chase. Like a hare . . . I'll even give you a few moments to get a good lead."

Slaver from the hound's mouth hit the dirt path, hissing like some strange poison.

There was no way he'd be able to outrun it. He looked around: nowhere to hide, no branches low enough to scramble into a tree. Swallowing hard, he tried it. "And then I had a sword."

Jack glanced around him: there were no weapons of any kind on the bristling grass. It hadn't worked.

The hound opened its blue-black lips, baying. If they were above-ground, Jack would expect that sound to summon some hunter to finish off a treed animal.

His heart raced as he thought about what he'd done when it worked. *Eyes. I closed my eyes.*

As it advanced, the beast seemed even more menacing. Its teeth weren't like regular dog's teeth—each tooth was jagged with tiny serrations.

Jack closed his eyes. *Even if it doesn't work, at least I won't see it as it eats me.* In his imagination, he pictured a sword, the one he'd seen most recently, Ivy's. "Then as the beast looked at the boy, it saw that he had a sword, a beautiful sword which could be wielded to stop the hound."

He flexed his empty hand. He opened his eyes, hoping the sword was at his feet. It didn't.

"So, Jack Merry, you've saved me the work of finding you." Ivy stepped in front of him, between him and the beast. "What're doing with one of the Huntsmen's hounds?"

The hound in question hadn't moved.

"Ivy!" He might still be angry and hurt, but he didn't mean to summon Ivy into danger. She didn't need to get injured by the beast. But then again, if her life were tied to his, his being eaten by the beast would be pretty dangerous to her anyhow. "I'm sorry. I just meant to make a sword . . . Just give it here. You don't need it . . ."

"Can you fight, Jack?" Her voice sounded like she was but a moment from laughter. "Do you know swordplay, then?"

Growling, like the rumble of an earth tremor, sounded in the beast's throat.

Jack stepped backwards, trying to tug Ivy with him. "No, but . . ."

"Shall I dispatch the hound then?" She didn't look at him while she spoke, her gaze fixed on the beast. "This mortal is with me; he wears my mark."

"He'll run just the same." Its tongue licked its muzzle. "I've not caught a mortal in . . . oh, a fortnight, I believe it's been."

"Jack Merry?"

"Yes."

"Tell the hound why you wandered into his path without me."

Jack glanced past Ivy to the hound. "She didn't tell me that my telling her a story made the sword in her hand, and she *could have*. She lied."

"By mortal standards . . . not by the rules of the realm." She sighed. "Tell him about before that, what happened to the Twitches."

"In the tunnel, I told her a story about a princess with a sword who had the strength of a score of Red-Caps. I guess, she . . ."

"Slew them, Jack. I stopped or slew them so they didn't rend us limb from limb."

Jack had to fight the nausea that threatened. "Right . . . She 'slew' them, and umm, here we are, but I got angry and . . ."

"The strength of a score of Red-Caps?" It interrupted, tilting its head and peering at Jack. Its red eyes flashed darker. "Imagine that."

Ivy lowered her sword, pointing the tip to the ground, but still holding tight to the hilt. "Yes, imagine."

The hound settled back on its haunches. "Did you think it wise to let him wander off?"

The beast went from threatening to chastising Ivy for "letting" him walk away. Jack was growing less afraid by the moment and simultaneously angrier again. "If she'd have been truthful--like she promised . . ."

"By the rules of the realm, I've broken no vow," she murmured, still not looking away from the beast.

Jack could swear the hound grinned at them.

"Suppose you'll not let me chase him, Princess?"

Ivy shook her head.

"I've already summoned the Huntsmen. If you don't behead me, you know I'm bound to tell of this," it said, sounding surprisingly calm despite the import of its words. "I don't fancy being beheaded."

"I know."

Open-mouthed, Jack looked from Ivy to the beast. *Absolutely inane, that's what this world was!* "So, you're going to kill him?"

"Perhaps, Jack, unless there's a better way you can offer. The hounds are all quite mad--Mother's gift to them, you know. He would likely have mauled you terrible bad once he caught you. Lest the Hunt reached you first, they'd have ridden over you, sliced your mortal to skin to shreds with their steed's hooves." Ivy glanced at him, half-smiling. "Have you a solution?"

Mauled him, severed a limb, trampled by some strange horses--yes, Jack suspected that had he not been able to summon Ivy it would've been quite awful. Still, killing the creature as they stood talking seemed pretty awful too. "I do."

Ivy had resuming watching the beast.

Jack leaned in and whispered, "Are there limits to this little skill of mine?"

"I've not a clue, Jack Merry." She lifted the sword as the beast--for no discernable reason--stood. "It was but a legend. I've watched you these past seasons, but I'd not known if the legends were truth. Until you gave me the skills to vanquish the Twitches . . ."

The dog's slaver was falling, hissing, onto the ground again. It looked vicious, but in its eyes Jack thought—*believed*—he saw hope for an answer.

He closed his eyes. "The princess and her friend came upon a beast, but the beast didn't truly mean them harm."

"Hound, Jack, he's one of the Huntsmen's hounds. Mother finds them more . . . useful if they're prone to fits of madness. Says it keeps the folk wary, obedient."

"Well, although the hound had been plagued by a madness that made him vicious, as the princess looked at the hound," he paused, adding in an undertone, "Look at the hound, Ivy."

"I am."

"As she looked at the hound, she saw the cause of his madness and his wrath. It was a . . . a parasite, sitting ever so still on the hound's head." Jack pictured it, a big green insect, bloated like a tick. It stared at them, unable to hide itself. "The hound stayed quite still as the princess gently dislodged the parasite."

"I have, Jack."

"Once it was gone . . . is it gone?" He heard the sound of her sword slicing the air, a crunching sound, and then silence. "Then, the hound had no desire to wound the princess or any she cared about. It knew that they meant it no harm."

At first it was silent, but then the hound spoke. "So, the legends were true."

"Open your eyes, Jack Merry."

He did, and glancing down, saw the foul insect that he'd made. That, at least, had worked. "So, now what?"

"I feel well." The hound grinned. "But I must report your mortal to the Huntsmen. They'll be most interested in his coming here."

"It didn't work." Despite being angry that he'd been misled, Jack had been rather pleased to have such a skill. Now, though, it appeared to have failed. He felt foolish for having spoken so and Ivy still needing to behead the hound. "I could try again. . ."

"It worked just fine." Ivy nudged the bloated insect with her sword tip. "The hound must tell the Huntsmen, to do otherwise would be to go against his very nature, his function."

"I'll tell them I owe a boon to him on account of his gift." The hound shrugged, an odd gesture for a dog. "I bear no malice towards you. In truth, I am humbled by your gift. I shall tell my masters of your gift and your honor."

Ivy nodded. "It is a fair trade."

"Though we are used for callous deeds, it was not always so in the realm." The hound looked past them, as if it saw something that Jack could not fathom. Then he turned that red gaze to Jack. "Perhaps this too might change."

Then, it fled--running so quickly that it was gone before Jack could even speak. He shook his head.

No chance of outrunning that!

TURNING TO FACE HIM, IVY SAID, "WELL, THEN, WHERE SHALL we go from here? Are you for breaking your vow and going back above-ground?"

Jack sputtered, "You are absolutely impossible. You do realize that, don't you?"

Choosing to ignore his remark, Ivy started down the path. He'd follow or he wouldn't. "I understand that your world's rules are that I should've told you sooner."

He followed, kicking a rock and scuffing his feet on the path. "Is your whole family as difficult as you are?"

If only he knew.

Ivy shook her head. "Not at all, Jack. I'm the reasonable one."

"I'm having trouble believing that." He had caught up and was keeping pace with her.

"Truly." She'd taken a turn behind a vine laden copse of trees, gesturing at a field hidden behind it.

Fat drops of water were being sucked from the soil, drawn into clouds that were bloated and heavy with water. Plants withered, crackling into dead things. Perhaps, he'd understand if he saw.

Not that she understood, but she knew it was real. She knew it was reason enough to break the *geas,* to accept the curse, to mislead Jack. It was reason enough to do much that could lead to trouble.

As Jack looked on, she pointed to the distance where they could see the edge of another field. There, clouds were dripping a sulfurous liquid that smoked and sizzled as it landed on the ground.

"Where are we?" Jack's face looked sickly as he turned to face her.

"My home, Jack." Ivy made her voice as empty, as flat as she could. "Mother's having a bad day."

"But . . ." His gaze went past her, to the waterfall, and he stumbled.

She didn't want to turn--she'd seen it too many times--but she did. Ghastly green sludge glopped down. At the foot of the water-fall, wan water-maidens gasped.

Jack went toward them, and Ivy had no choice but follow.

Jonquil darted from one gasping woman to the next, touching each one's lips until they were all breathing somewhat regularly.

Clematis fluttered over and nodded, once, like a sage old woman. "You did that, gave her the gift that saved these." She gestured towards the water-maidens with a dip of her head. "They'll suffer less because of it."

"What if she weren't here?" He dropped to his knees.

"Not to fear, Jack Merry. They wouldn't all die, even if our Jonquil weren't here." Ivy glanced at the water-maidens: long hair knotted with clumps of green sludge, eyes wide with terror as they clung to the tall grasses on the bank. She turned away, feeling sick inside. "They'd suffocate until the Queen thought to repair the waters, perhaps this eve, perhaps later. She usually remembers before too long passes. Most would survive."

Jack didn't answer; he closed his eyes. "The princess gazed at the water, and she saw that it was suddenly purer than it had ever been. It was glorious--perfect for the creatures that thrived there."

Tears slid down Ivy's cheeks as she watched that thick, noxious sludge turn to clear waters. The water-maidens were slipping off the banks, laughing.

Ivy whispered, "It is glorious, Jack Merry."

But Jack wasn't done. "And the poisonous rain and drought were gone. The fields were perfect, ripe with life. Fresh . . ."

"Wheats and sun-fruits."

"Right, wheats and sun-fruits flourished . . . as if they'd been growing all along." Jack's voice became whispery. He swayed.

The clouds vanished, and wheat sprung up.

Ivy steadied Jack.

"Enough." Jonquil was patting Jack's cheek. Her voice sounded awfully loud for such a tiny creature. "Stop, now."

Jack toppled, eyes still firmly closed.

"Jack?" Ivy shook his shoulder.

He didn't move.

Myriad panicked thoughts raced through Ivy's mind. She kept shaking Jack, repeating his name in a fervent plea, "Be well. Please be well, Jack Merry."

Then, Jack opened his mouth and snored.

Clematis snorted in laughter.

And as tears streamed down her face, Ivy began to laugh too, because sometimes the choice is to laugh or simply break into tiny, tiny pieces.

Chapter 8: In which the past is revealed

⁂

When Jack woke up, Jonquil was perched on a rock beside him. Her knees were bent, and tiny bare feet were sliding back and forth over the grey surface of the rock with a soft shuffling sound. She hummed to herself, sounding rather like a purring cat.

He propped his head up on one hand. "Is there more to that song?"

"Not sure. Mother used to hum it when we were ill." She glanced at him. "I find it calming." She paused and stared at him. "You're doing well, Jack Merry. The realm is fortunate to have you here."

Jack didn't bother trying to make sense of what she said; things here always seemed so serious. He stretched and asked, "How long did I sleep?"

"Long enough." She fluttered off towards a slow-moving lizard, dipping down to stroke the creature's scaled head as she passed. "I'd better tell the others. They've been like mothers worrying over you."

Jack didn't point out that she was obviously hovering, too. Closing his eyes, Jack thought of having a mother that hummed when he wasn't well. The closest he'd come to such care were the stolen visits from Widow Stonewell. Her face was wrinkled even then. When she smiled, Jack thought her skin would crack like a dry river bed after a drought.

He thought of how she'd stroke his hair, snagging her calloused hand. It wasn't quite an embrace, but when she'd slip in the back door, surprisingly quiet for her age, it was her custom. Then again, so was her refusing to take him to her home. Remembering those moments was bittersweet.

The widow leaned closer so that her dark dress brushed against his legs. "I saw the good Parson at Oldaker's place, so I thought I'd stop by."

Jack looked at her; hoping his pleading would finally work. "Take me to live with you. I swear I'd be good, better than I am now."

Her face crumpled, for just an instant. "Jackie boy, come on now. You know I can't do that." She patted his cheek. "The Good folk wanted you to live here, with the Parson. I'm not one to question their ways."

"Parson says there's no such thing." Jack truly thought she was kind, despite what the Parson said about her 'superstitious ways.' "He says I'm not to talk to you, that you work against his efforts to save me."

Widow Stonewell snorted. "The Parson's a good man, but he doesn't know everything. No one does. Remember that, Jackie. There's more out there than what we see, more than we can understand..."

Jack nodded, willing to agree to whatever she wanted.

"When you arrived . . . It was a beautiful thing, Jack. The one that brought you to us was terrible afraid. She was like a wild deer, frozen and trembling as she watched from the trees." Widow Stonewell sighed, and her eyes shone with the glimmer of tears. She always got teary when she talked about the night Jack was brought to the Parson. "A beautiful thing she was--a faery. Her hair glowed like there was fire caught in every strand of it. And she had these big leafy winged that she fluttered as she crept to the Parson's door; then, once she saw him come and lift you in his arms, she was gone. Just gone. Like I'd dreamt her."

Jack shook his head. He wanted to believe her, wanted to think that some strange faery woman left him at the Parson's door--only because she'd

*had no choice--though she'd loved him. He'd watched the children in the
town with their parents--mothers' fussing over tiny falls and fathers'
sweeping children into the air. Laughter and proud looks, those were things
the Parson didn't offer.*

*Widow Stonewell settled into one of the Parson's uncomfortable chairs.
"So . . . what does our good Parson have you doing on this fine day?"*

*"It's awful." He scowled at the parchment where he'd been trying,
futilely, to replicate the Parson's precise script. "I don't want to learn to
draw letters."*

*"Aah, Jackie," she lowered her already whispery voice. "Believe me,
boy, learning script leads to reading . . . Once that happens it's like opening
a door where you didn't even know there was one." She squeezed his arm.
"You're special, boy, and even as the Parson might not say it, he knows it
too. You'll see one day. They'll all see."*

Jack hadn't ever understood why the Widow visited him in
secrecy, but he was thankful for the little kindness she offered. It
was far more than anyone else had given him. Sometimes it still
hurt that she'd refused his years of begging to let him live with
her, to be loving when the town watched.

She'd simply say, "It's not what the Good Folk wanted, and if I
offer too much notice where the Parson can see . . . Well, it's
simply not wise."

Even now, after the Parson had given up on Jack, Widow
Stonewell clung to her belief. Nothing would sway her from
abiding by "the Good Folk's wisdom."

"Are you well, Jack Merry?"

Jack opened his eyes. Ivy was standing beside him, her hair
illuminated by the artificial light of the meadow so it looked like
hot coals. She smiled, tentatively.

When he didn't answer, she reached down to brush her hand
over his forehead. "Jack?"

"You said you'd watched me for years."

"I did." Her gaze was steadily on him. "But I've not made
trouble for you. Not once."

"Why?"

She looked puzzled--eyes widened, a small furrow on her brow. "Well, it's not right to do so. I know that mortals tell such tales, but truly we're not all like that. There's some that--"

"No. I mean, why did you watch me?" He looked at her; she appeared to be of a similar age as him.

She can't be, can she?

Gently, he prompted again, "Why did you watch me?"

She tilted her head, and Jack thought again how like some forest creature she was. "Well, I wasn't sure if that man was a good caretaker. The other mortals asked him for wisdom, and they seemed to regard him well, but one never knows."

The more she said, the more Jack felt sick. Surely, she couldn't be his *mother*. She was too young. He kept his voice as calm as he could manage, and asked, "So you wanted to be sure that the man who had me was a good man?"

Her face lit up, seemingly pleased. "If he weren't a kind man, I'd have taken you away from him. I swear it, Jack."

"Because you had picked him and felt responsible?" Jack's mouth was dry.

She frowned. "I'd thought of bringing you back home, but it wasn't safe. I couldn't protect you."

"You're too young . . . you can't be my . . . mother?" He couldn't form a clear thought, staring at her.

Her black eyes widened. "No!"

He let out a sigh of relief. He wanted a family, but he didn't think he wanted Ivy to be his mother.

"Time moves differently above-ground. It was but half of a year ago when I saw your parents hide you." She shivered, rubbing her hands briefly over her arms as if to warm them. "The Hunt strikes terror in everyone, but they--mortals though they were-- resisted long enough to tuck you into a hollow, and I couldn't let you there. There are things less frightening than the Hunt, and animals and . . . I did what I could."

The bells chimed then. Like pure silver this time, rich and clear.

ᔥ

"YOU SAW MY PARENTS?" JACK WAS WATCHING HER, LOOKING AT her intently.

"Yes," she whispered. Though it was several turns of the moon, she felt cold terror at the back of her neck as if it were but last eve. "I saw them, but I couldn't . . . they paused near where I hid."

He patted the ground beside him. "Tell me."

She shook her head. It was already growing dim. "We cannot stay here. The hound will've told the Huntsmen of your presence." Holding out her hand, she hoped he'd listen. Though she didn't tell him, she was weary and the thought of a battle, with even one Huntsmen, made her want to whimper.

He crossed his arms, looking like a petulant child, like he'd often looked when she'd spied him with the Parson. "Ivy, I have spent my whole life knowing nothing, *nothing* about my life other than the Widow's claims of seeing some faery girl deliver me to the Parson's door."

"The Widow's a wise woman." Ivy nodded, hand still outstretched.

"You know her?" Jack gaped, looking less happy by the moment. "She knew you all this time?"

Ivy gripped his hand, tugging him to his feet. "Please, Jack Merry." She looked around, seeing the Ellyllon hovering nearby. With a motion, she called them closer. "I'll tell you as much as I can. Even if it means coming above-ground after seeking audience with the Queen . . . if there's an after."

Hoping her horse would come, she whistled. She'd fashioned a hasty braid, and water-steeds were a picky lot.

"You can tell me more as we ride." Jack released her hand and stepped in front of her. "Your word, Ivy. I'll stay with you in this 'strife' of yours, but I have questions you can answer. You owe me that much."

Though she thought it strange that he needed answers to what was--to him--a lifetime ago, she nodded. "I'll speak of what I know, but there's not much to say."

"It's more than I know now." He stepped closer to her horse, raising his hand and offering a piece of green-birch fruit.

While the horse was distracted by its treat, Ivy looped the new braid over it and climbed astride. "So be it."

Jack nodded once and climbed up.

Once Jack was seated behind her, they were off again.

§&

THOUGH HE'D DREAMT OF HAVING ANSWERS TO HIS QUESTIONS for most of his life, Jack found himself struggling to form even the simplest query now that the chance was upon him. "What happened to my parents?"

"I found you there, in the tree where your mortal mother put you." Ivy paused, as if she weren't sure how much to say. "I couldn't leave you there."

She'd deftly avoided his real question, so Jack repeated, "What happened to them?"

She sighed in a long whoosh, and he realized it was her way of letting on that she was displeased. So, he just waited.

"Oh, Jack Merry, I don't know." She looked back over her shoulder, and her dark eyes were sorrowful. "The Hunt . . . they're a terrible force, and I couldn't . . . I couldn't go after them."

"Would you have?"

"I doubt it." She shook her head just a little, sending white tendrils snaking across his forearm. "I was hiding, Jack. I'm no match for The Hunt. The Huntsmen have ridden longer than I've drawn breath. They say, those that've lived to say, that the touch of the horse's breath will rot your flesh right from the bone."

She dropped back to silence, staring down the path with a vigilance that reminded him of the dangers they were no doubt heading towards.

He could see them, not their faces, but he could picture them running from strange terrors. His voice was rough as he asked, "Why were they chasing my parents?"

"They weren't, not really. It just . . . The Hunt roams. It's simply the way things are."

Over Ivy's shoulder, Jack could see her hands: one was clenched into a fist around the reins, the other rested on the hilt of her sword.

He felt badly that she was upset, but he kept on. "So, you found me after they were gone?"

She nodded.

"And you decided to take me to safety?" Jack couldn't remember ever feeling quite this way, like laughing and crying at the same time. He'd finally learned of his parents, but from Ivy's response he had little hope they were still alive. "Tell me."

And so, she did.

After she dropped to the forest floor, Ivy heard the cry from the hollow in the tree. She knew, before she even touched it that there was no way she'd leave the squalling thing behind.

She yanked the twigs and moss out of the hollow, and lifted that bundle tucked behind them.

The cloth around the mortal babe was filthy, so she took down a net of spider-silk and a few strands of moonlight to fashion a cloth to wrap around it. It was hastily fashioned glamour: sure to fade away once morning's light touched it, but till then it'd keep the child warm.

She'd been in the town before, so she knew the way.

First, she'd stopped at the Widow's door; she seemed a good woman-- leaving butter or milk on her step, not like some mortals.

She peered in the Widow's window.

"Parson's a good man," the Widow was saying, hands on her hips, scowl on her face. "Give him time, Glenna."

"Bah!" A woman paced, flailing a body as thin as Cerridan's limbs during a drought. "Fool, that's what he is."

"He's a wise man, just not used to our ways." The Widow sighed, looking out her window.

Ivy ducked behind the hedge, holding the babe tight to her chest.

The door opened and the thin woman came outside. "I'm starting to think you're daft, sister."

She stomped down the planks in ill-fitting shoes.

Silently, the Widow stared into the shadows, a half-smile on her lips. "He's good for the town. He wants schooling for the young ones, and he even . . ."

"Enough." The thin woman held up a hand. "I'll talk to him, but I don't like him."

Still looking around the yard, the Widow murmured, "I don't know that I like him either, sister, but he cares for the town. That's enough for me."

Ivy kept a hand over the infant's mouth as she watched the Widow hobble off, pausing to gaze into the shadows every few steps.

Ivy stayed out of sight a moment longer, gazing down at the child. "Well, little one, I suppose the Widow'd know who to trust."

So, Ivy wound her way through the shadows to the Parson's doorstep. He'd seemed a good man when she'd seen him, though she knew he claimed the fey folk weren't real.

A light rain fell as she stood outside the door, debating. Finally, she set the babe on the Parson's doorstep and rapped on the door until she heard him approach.

Then she hid behind a tree and watched him lift the child in his arms.

"Come out," he called, holding the child gently, though awkwardly. "I'll listen, whatever it is." He waited, and then called again, "I'll leave the latch open, if you decide to come in."

Ivy smiled. He was a good man. Looking up, she saw the Widow, staring open-mouthed at her.

And she fled into the wood, hoping she'd not see the Hunt or anything else.

Jack said nothing at first. He wasn't sure what to think. His parents were probably dead; the Parson was chosen by sheer chance. It wasn't as if everything he'd thought or wondered was untrue, but it wasn't altogether true either.

He rested his forehead on Ivy's shoulder. "Later, when I'm able, can I ask more?"

"Yes," she whispered, turning her head so her cheek brushed his forehead. "I tried. Truly I did."

"I know." He didn't move, taking comfort in her friendship for a moment. "And when I'm able, I'll tell you--without saying 'thank you'--how much it means."

He felt her brief nod before she turned back to watching the path.

And they continued in silence.

Chapter 9: In which the Bollynoggins appear

꧁꧂

Daisy had kept herself—and her sisters—well out of sight while Ivy and Jack talked. From the cover of trees, she waited patiently. Beside her, Clematis danced down the limb, stabbing the air with that infernal dagger.

Repressing a sigh, Daisy looked back at Ivy and Jack. It was good for them to reveal their truths and worries. Trust would vanish with secrets untold.

"Are we going?" Jonquil cuddled a tree-frog, stroking the poisonous skin with a comfort that few in the realm would dare. After so many exposures to toxins, she seemed immune to most everything.

Seeing as the conversation had stopped, Daisy nodded. "Let's."

Clematis stepped off the branch, wings stilled, falling through the air. Then, at the last possible moment she flapped her wings rapidly.

"Looks fun, don't you think?" Jonquil had her back turned as she settled the poisonous frog on the branch.

"No, I don't." Daisy shook her head. "She's a terror."

Jonquil wiped her hands on several leaves, smearing poison

evenly over the pale green surfaces; then, she folded those poison-covered leaves into tiny pouches and tucked them in her pockets. "She's not as foolhardy as she pretends."

With a grin, Jonquil stepped forward into thin air, looking entirely too much like their baby sister. But she wasn't even halfway down when a great white egret swooped beneath her.

With a loud war whoop, two stocky Bollynoggins standing on the bird's back grabbed Jonquil in their arms. Their strangely muscular bodies twisted as they settled her between them. "Daisy? Are you riding with us?"

"As you're here, I don't suppose there's a choice."

In perfect synchronicity, the Bollynoggins winked. A third Bollynoggin, Hagan, steered the egret right up under the limb. It slowed down, and Hagan grinningly offered, "I could lasso you."

Daisy stepped forward, using her wings to glide towards the bird. "I could sic my sister on you."

"Hey, Matty, she thinks you're a match for us." Then, with their usual enthusiasm, two Bollynoggins wrapped arms around her and tugged her on the bird's back. "Hold tight."

At a word from the driver, the bird sped up.

"No fair!" Clematis buzzed alongside the bird, straining to keep up and failing quickly.

The Bollynoggins laughed, lilting piping sounds like swamp-insects. One of them pointed to the ground. "Grams thought you'd like a more stylish model."

Below them, a vibrant green serpent waited. A tiny bridle went over the snake's head; attached to it were woven reins.

Clematis shrieked as she plummeted downward again. "I can ride her?"

Hagan snorted. "You can try."

JACK LOOKED UP AS AN EGRET SWOOPED BY. ON ITS BACK WERE

Daisy, Jonquil, and several tiny creatures that seemed to be howling.

He nudged Ivy and pointed. "Are they snatching the Ellyllon or giving them a ride?"

Ivy shook her head. "Despite how much Daisy will complain later, the Bollynoggins mean no harm." She called out, "Shall we follow?"

The Bollynoggins circled back on their egret, landing on a hedge along the path.

A small green man, who was clad in bark armor and a moss vest, bowed briefly. "Grandmother Nogs sends greetings, Princess, but she'd like to talk to the Ellyllon in private."

Though they hadn't spoken, all three Bollynoggins had glanced at him, so Jack bowed his head briefly. "Only if Daisy and Jonquil are fine with it."

Jonquil opened her mouth to answer, but a Bollynoggin quickly clamped a hand over her mouth. Another did the same with Daisy.

The Bollynoggins exchanged grins, looking fierce despite their size. "And what if they aren't?"

"Well, then, I suppose it'll go poorly for you." Jack offered them the most unpleasant smile he could. "No one will hurt the Ellyllon."

Daisy stepped on the Bollynoggin's foot, and he let go of her.

She sighed. "We're quite fine with this lot, Jack Merry. Despite their manners--"

"We have manners, Hagan!" One of the Bollynoggins interrupted. "Do you hear her? Manners."

Jonquil nudged a Bollynoggin in the ribs. "Sorry, Ivy. We'll catch up before you reach the moat."

"It's all good, Jack." Clematis--standing on the back of a serpent, holding tiny reins in her hand--waved cheerily.

As Jack gaped, the serpent sped off with Clematis on its back.

The Bollynoggins on the egret let out a series of bird-like

wails. "Come on, faster. Matty's going to beat us if this is all the faster we're going..."

And as Jack watched, the bird took flight again with the Ellyllon and Bollynoggins swaying on its back.

❦

IVY LAUGHED AT THE TRULY BEFUDDLED EXPRESSION ON JACK'S face. It was a fine improvement over the sorrowful look he'd been wearing earlier. "The Bollynoggins are good folk, Jack, and Grandmother Nogs loves the Ellyllon as if they were her own."

"She was riding a snake. And the Bollynoggins..." He shook his head. "Even those things that seem harmless don't seem very nice."

She thought on it for a moment; she could see where he'd think that. "It's not that the folk aren't 'nice,' just perhaps things aren't as clear here as they are above-ground."

"Daisy didn't look happy." He looked in the direction they'd gone, worry clear on his face.

"Daisy's happier with the Bollynoggins than she'll admit. They make her laugh; they make her do truly foolish things. It's good for her."

"What if there's a hound or what if your sister..."

Ivy turned to look at him. "They're safer with the Bollynoggins than with us. Ada doesn't consider them as a threat." She smiled, glad the Ellyllon would get a rest before they reached the Queen's presence. "And Grandmother Nogs won't let them come to any harm. We'll see them when we wake."

After a moment he nodded; then he frowned. "Where will we sleep?"

Ivy could hear the faint sounds of the town ahead of them. She was loath to admit it to Jack, but she was far from sure they'd be welcome. As she mused on it, she suspected Grandmother Nogs had come to the same realization. "Pwca Vale is just ahead.

Ada will've passed this way, but she's not the only daughter of the court."

"Should we expect much trouble?"

"That, Jack Merry, is quite a good question." Returning her attention to the path, she watched with growing fear as they came closer to Pwca Vale. "One never knows, not here."

᠀

AS THEY ENTERED PWCA VALE, JACK THOUGHT YET AGAIN OF how truly unprepared he was for the sheer scope of Ivy's world. Without the Ellyllon and their ready answers, he was left all too aware that there was no way to tell friend from foe, normal behavior from threatening.

A lanky creature sauntered by on legs that seemed to spring and stretch like they had no bones in them. It grinned, or perhaps scowled. Not knowing what was best, Jack aimed to look somber.

Everywhere he looked vines hung down like invitations to climb, and from among the leaves tiny pink-eyed creatures flashed feral smiles. Overhead, birds that looked familiar mingled with winged things that he'd no words to even describe—like giant slugs with a clear shell over top so that their innards showed.

Through it all, Ivy kept her back straight and her fingers on the hilt of her sword.

"Stay close when we stop." Ivy's voice was a strained whisper, punctuated by her somber replies to the creatures' myriad calls of, "Be welcome, Princess."

"Right. Close." Jack watched as a small cluster of goat-legged women stamped their hooves as Ivy called out greetings to them. "Anything else?"

She glanced toward the hooved women and in a low voice said, "Hope the Glaistigs aren't quarrelsome and that my status is enough that Ada's spies don't act outright."

The goat-women hadn't looked away. They stared and spoke

amongst themselves all the while. Various weapons decorated their costumes--curved blades and heavy cudgels. Even without the weapons, they were daunting--muscular and menacing--and strangely appealing. Several flashed smiles at him, acknowledging his perusal. Jack looked away and repressed a shiver at the idea of Ivy's fighting them. "Is anyone here friendly?"

Ivy didn't answer. She lifted a hand in greeting to a deer with the face of a man. He didn't respond. "If the Vale has become . . . untenable for us, the best we can hope is that we've enough allies to stall our enemies."

She continued to answer greetings, curtseys, and bows, but she kept her eyes as watchful as when they'd crossed the Twitches' tunnel.

Jack leant forward so his mouth was near her ear. "Is it wise to stop here?"

"We don't have much choice. We need to rest, and there's nowhere else near that'd be any safer." She stopped the water-horse in front of another immense tree. Lichens stuck out in a spiral pattern, like steps that'd grown by chance.

Looking back at him, Ivy offered a small smile and murmured, "Slide down first, Jack Merry."

Silently, he complied.

"If you would . . ." She handed him her sword, hilt-first so her fingers slid along the steel blade. Her skin reddened, and she held her hand out so as anyone could see the ugly burn.

And Jack was sure they did see it. A rather emaciated man grinned and nodded his head, another creature with scaled wings and glinting talons hissed--perhaps in empathy, perhaps in hunger.

"My pleasure." Jack held out his free hand to Ivy. He closed his eyes briefly and lifted his voice. "And with as little time as it took to draw a breath, the princess' hand was healed once more."

He opened his eyes and winked at her.

Her eyes widened in surprise, but only for a fraction of a

moment. Then she took his hand and was on the ground beside him, holding her now-healed hand out for her sword.

From the looks they were receiving, Jack suspected the murmured conversations weren't all friendly ones. He slid the hilt into her waiting grasp. "I am at your command, my lady."

With one of those eerie laughs, Ivy moved in front of him. "Indeed, Jack Merry?"

"Indeed." He kept his false smile in place as he followed her through the crowd. "At your word and your side."

☙

As the egret neared Grandmother Nogs' Swamp, the Bollynoggins yelled, "Incoming!"

Two brothers each wrapped strong arms round Jonquil and Daisy and leapt from the egret's back.

As they hurtled towards the boggy water, Jonquil heard Daisy shriek and spout several creative threats. Not far above the water, but with still enough time to avoid getting wet, Hagan let go. "Flap away, girlie."

She angled up as he splashed into the water.

Daisy zipped over, scowling fiercely, hands on her hips. "The whole colony is filled with menaces! As if Clematis wasn't headache enough . . ."

Hagan surfaced with a loud whoop. Floating on his back, he stared up at her.

Biting her cheek to keep from laughing, Jonquil waited.

Predictable to a fault, Daisy announced, "Hmph! Infants have more sense than you, Hagan Nogs!"

Hagan merely grinned and kicked his feet in the water.

"Daisy . . ." Jonquil pointed to the shore where Clematis had just stopped her racing snake.

But Daisy took no notice. She zipped down to the surface. "Do you hear me? One of these times . . ."

"I missed you." Hagan reached up and wrapped his arms around Daisy's middle; laughing, he pulled her into the water. "Even your scowling face."

When Daisy resurfaced, she was still berating him, but her eyes were twinkling.

Jonquil couldn't help it: she laughed at the bedraggled pair. "I'll see to Clematis."

"I'll come." Daisy struggled to get free of Hagan's grasp, smacking his arm lightly. Strands of bog-grass tangled in Daisy's hair and brown water sluiced off her face. "We should see what Grandmother Nogs wants."

"Stay." Jonquil smiled gently at her. Hagan's foolishness never failed to cheer Daisy. "We'll all sit down and talk after eating."

Still, Daisy started to protest, "But . . ."

Grinning, Hagan shoved her under water again. "We'll be up soon."

As Jonquil touched down on the spongy shore, Grandmother Nogs stepped into view. Her patterned green skin and brown tufted hair made her hard to spot unless she chose to be seen. "Matty. Jonquil. Good of you to come see me."

Jonquil curtseyed. "Daisy is with us."

"I expected so." She smiled, a quick flash of softness as she looked over the swamp. "Hagan's been worse than a swarm of nettle-bees since I said you'd be by. Boy makes me tired." She looked up and nodded at one of her boys.

He rolled out a length of woven swamp-grass in front of her. After bowing to Grandmother Nogs and to Eamon, the captain of the guard, the young Bollynoggin left.

Grandmother Nogs settled her considerable girth on the horned toad that always followed her and crossed her ankles delicately. "We'll sit here where I can see Daisy too."

Jonquil sat down on the woven grass, listening to Eamon issue orders to the retinue of bodyguards. Six of the Bollynoggins—

armed with bows and a good supply of cactus-spike arrows--crept into the marshy weeds.

"Arth tells me you want a longbow, Matty." Grandmother Nogs rarely wasted time on trivial talk. She made approving noises deep in her throat. "Longbow's a good choice for you. I watched your practice with the other tools. You're too slight for the mace."

"Yes, Grandmother Nogs." Clematis plopped down next to Jonquil on the swamp-grass.

Jonquil stretched, twisting her arms out behind her and rolling her shoulders, and waited.

Grandmother Nogs tapped a hand on the toad's bumpy head. "The dagger's nice, but you still need to be so close. What do you think?"

"I think keeping Clematis out of close combat would ease Daisy's nerves." Jonquil pretended not to hear Clematis' snort. Her sister might be irritated, but she'd not speak out of turn with Grandmother Nogs. "And I think she'd benefit from the need for focus in using the bow."

"You're as clever as always." Grandmother Nogs gazed out over her swamp. "It's a good skill to have. Yes, indeed." She sighed as she sat and stared. "Troubles come towards you."

"With sisters like mine, trouble's common enough." Jonquil wrinkled her nose at Clematis.

Grandmother Nogs sighed like music flowing through hollow logs. "I well remember, but it's not your sisters that started this trouble, is it? You forget how much I see."

Jonquil held Grandmother Nogs' gaze. "I still say I am right in my path. Things need changing."

With wide eyes, Clematis looked back and forth between Jonquil and Grandmother Nogs.

With a barely perceptible rise in her voice, Grandmother Nogs asked the question she'd been asking since Jonquil had told Ivy the legends, "Are you still willing to risk so much?"

Standing up, Jonquil moved in front of Grandmother Nogs and held out her hands. "If I didn't try, what risk then?" She took those swamp-slick hands in her own. "I've not forgotten *any* of the legends. If we don't do this, what might we lose?"

Grandmother Nogs stood up. "I'll think on it. From the murmurs I hear, it's a decision that needs made soon. I'm not happy about it. Not at all." Then, Grandmother Nogs let go of Jonquil's hands and made a signal in the air.

Soundless as always, the guards surrounded them again.

"I'll send the boys to fetch you for the meal. You'll have my answer then." Grandmother Nogs turned to Clematis. "Come, Matty. We'll have Eamon take you to the shop. Jonquil is quite right on this at least: a longbow is a fine choice."

Ignoring Clematis' beseeching look, Jonquil curtseyed to the Bog Mother. "Until then."

Chapter 10: In which revolutions are hinted at

❧

Ivy tried not to flinch as Jorge came nearer. Not because of his red teeth or even the ominous axe on his stump-table, no, it was his moods that made her tense: Jorge was unpredictable on his best days.

"Princess." He spat to the side, sniffled a little, and glared at Jack. "What business bring you here?"

"I'm going to see the Queen, my Mother." She nudged Jack further behind her. The nearest vine-gnarlers were too far to reach him; the Glaistigs were still keeping their distance. For now, behind her was safest. "I am set for the Queen's presence."

"The Queen's Own came through not long ago." He squinted, opened and closed his mouth a few times, and finally made a choking noise in his throat. His scaled feet made scuffling noises as he trod on the wooden platform in front of his lodging tree. "Queen's Own *she* is."

"As am I." Ivy reached into her satchel and felt for a coin purse. It'd be quicker if she could look, but she was unwilling to take her gaze off Jorge. She doubted he'd bite her, but she wasn't certain. "Yet I pay my way."

He looked at her satchel, eyes glimmering with a green glow

now that she had mentioned paying. "Princesses needn't pay. Queen's Own say so."

"A gift then." Her fingers touched on the silver slivers in her satchel.

"Gifts . . . Her Own gave no gifts." He made a rattling noise in his chest again, like something was stuck in there and made his breathing harder than it should be. Maybe it was. No one in the realm was quite sure what Jorge was.

"I am the Queen's Own, and I call it fair to offer gifts." She pulled out the three pieces of silver, letting them clink together in her palm. "Leastways, among friends . . ."

A flop-eared girl with a short dagger darted forward and sniffed the silver. "True and spoken. Gifts of Princess. Good-good."

Jorge snarled at the girl. She hissed back, her twin tongues slashing out like tiny whips.

"Friends are fine to have." Ivy clutched the hilt of her sword with her free hand. "Indeed, I have many friends who've stood with me." She sighed. "Still and true, my sister knows that those who take coins might be tempted by bonds other than friendship."

"Gifts. Some folk give gifts to bind into other meetings." Jorge sniffled and spat again. "Not friends with little Princess. Trouble in such vows."

Vine-gnarlers dropped down and soaked fungus strips in the spittle. Their pincer-edged feet clacked together as they hurriedly gathered the spittle that'd go to make their poisoned darts. Then, they scurried back up the vines, chattering in that strange way of theirs. Once, Clematis had said that they were speaking, but their words were too fast to make sense to most folk.

"Just one night's rest and ample warning if you find a reason we need to leave here quickly." Ivy held the coins out again. Behind her she felt Jack move closer, and hoped that there wasn't another danger coming closer. "No orders from me, no terms of the next meeting, just this eve and we go on."

"Rest. Food. No vows for next meet." Jorge gargled, and held out his hand. "Gifts for this exchange."

Ivy curled her fingers around the silver. "And true warning should we need to leave sooner than planned. I cannot rest if I worry over our safety."

The flop-eared girl hissed and sidled near. "Guard you well." She nodded vigorously, her ears slapping her shoulders with a soft *thwack-thwack*. "Friends. No gift at all."

Jack whispered, with some panic in his tone, "If I might, Princess, I'd say that taking the deal now seems wise."

Thinking the same thing, Ivy murmured, "My vow it is so." Then, she turned back to see what troubled Jack. The goat-legged Glaistigs were stroking his hair and shoulders, stamping their feet and crowding close to him.

She looked at them, trying to figure which was the elder here. She studied the shorn circles with oghams carved in their hairy flanks, exposed by the long slits on the side of their traditional breeches. The symbols spelt out tales of their greatest feats or at least their clan names, but they moved too frequently for Ivy to decipher the words.

The tallest Glaistig shoved a younger one to the side, but the young one didn't retaliate.

Before Ivy could act, Jorge stepped in front of her. "Princess and her mortal rest now." He pointed into the tree-lodge. "Fiona," he tugged the flop-eared girl's hair and gargled, "Go with."

The flop-eared girl, Fiona, hissed. With a not-entirely-gentle headbutt, she herded Jack forward. "Pretty mortal." Her ears *thwack-thwacked* again as she nodded. "Keep safe."

"Yes, I'm sure you will." Stifling a yawn, Ivy stroked Fiona's head. "Friends then?"

Fiona nodded, *thwackthwackthwack*. "Friends and true."

"I'll remember it." Ivy yawned again, determined to ignore the snarling exchange between Jorge and the Glaistigs. A secure sleeping chamber sounded better than most anything she could think of.

🙋

CLEMATIS STRUGGLED TO KEEP UP WITH GRANDMOTHER NOGS. Sticks and vines cluttered the path, making wings useless and rather inconvenient. "Grandmother?"

The Bog Mother moved as if there were no obstacles in their low and winding path. She stepped forward without any obvious attention to what was before them, but her arms weren't scraped, nor were her pantaloons snagged.

"Grandmother Nogs!" Ignoring the dangling thistle-teeth creepers, Clematis rushed forward and gripped Grandmother Nogs' arm. "What's going on?"

The Bog Mother swiveled, a sorrowful look on her heavy features. "Matty child, I can't offer you the answers you seek." She slapped a bog-fly with a brief snarl as it came close to Clematis' bleeding arms. "Jonquil and I have spoken of the troubles for a long while. She knows the danger, but she still rushes forward."

"I don't understand . . ."

Grandmother Nogs murmured some almost-silent command and the guards slipped into the reeds again. She shook her head. "The Queen reigns over the realm. This is the way it's been for as long as any of us recall." She pausing, staring at a mottled brown rat that was trying futilely to fend off a pair of racing serpents. "Those that would change things . . . the cost can be too high. Jonquil knows this, but she still tries to convince me and mine to join a battle that is not ours."

"Jonquil? *My Jonquil?*"

Grandmother Nogs laughed, a smoky sound like wood-fires in the fog. "Jonquil is a girl with many secrets, Matty. She's not as meek as she lets you and Daisy think." She shook her head. "No,

Jonquil bides her time, thinking and planning. She's got a good heart, and a good cause too, but I'm getting too old to go out battling for changes, Matty-love."

Clematis opened and closed her mouth, soundlessly, like the water-maidens at the foul lake. *Jonquil?* She almost laughed at the thought. *My sweet sister, a revolutionary?* But as she stood there, watching the rat lose its fight, she had to admit that the thought of it wasn't entirely unbelievable. Jonquil might hold her tongue, but she was livid at the suffering of the creatures in the realm. "What does she want from you?"

Grandmother Nogs smiled, but it wasn't a gentle smile. Her sharp teeth glimmered in the green glow of bog-lights. "Why, she wants me to call in my favours with those that I hold sway over. She wants me and mine to follow your Ivy if the Queen insists on a fight. And she will, you know. She and Ada aren't simply going to bow down because Ivy asks it of them."

"Fight?" Clematis started.

But the Bog Mother went on as if Clematis hadn't spoken. "I am not willing to risk my boys, Matty. You must understand. The bog . . . the Queen and Ada do not bother us, not now, but if we help you . . ." She sighed, loudly, and gestured at the musty darkness. Strange songs echoed over the water, slithering things and splashing things. It was a soothing, albeit eerie, music. "I have much to lose."

And in that moment, Clematis saw something that she'd never seen before: the Bog Mother was afraid. With all her years of wisdom and tangled alliances, she was still afraid.

"Matty," Grandmother Nogs whispered, harsh and low. "Stay with us. Talk to your sisters. If you try . . ."

"You've been family to us, and maybe Daisy might stay, but Jonquil won't. She'll go with Ivy and Jack on the morrow." Clematis lowered her voice. "The legends--they're true. Jack Merry has the Queen's very gift. He made a sword for Ivy, fashioned it without even a struggle. He gave Jonquil the healing touch."

At first, Grandmother Nogs did not reply. They stood there, silent in the shadows of the bog-grass, listening to far off cries of musk-roans and wiskins. Finally, the Bog Mother nodded briskly. "So be it. Jonquil will go, but you and Daisy . . . Just think on it."

Clematis looked at her. She had been there for them so often, a family when they needed one. "I'll talk to Daisy. Maybe Hagan should try to talk to her, too?"

At that suggestion, Grandmother Nogs laughed. "Maybe. It might be all she needs to convince her to leave sooner though." She gestured that they were moving forwards. "Let's see about your bow, then. We've a little time before our meal."

And with that, the guards circled them once more and they were off as if nothing had changed, but to Clematis it felt as if everything had.

Chapter 11: In which Ivy and Jack leave Pwca Vale

✦❦✦

I t seemed she'd no sooner fallen asleep than Ivy woke with a stone-hard hand clamped over her mouth.

The scant light from the glowflies in the room wasn't enough to allow Ivy to see her captor's face, but the musky scent of fur left no doubt. *Glaistig, and more than one.* They never traveled alone these days, preferring the comfort of sister-in-arms too much to risk losing one of their ever-dwindling herd.

"Shh, little one . . ."

Ivy tried to turn her head to see Jack, but the Glaistig's grip allowed for no movement.

"Come now. Time is swift, but we shall be swifter." The Glaistig slid her free arm under Ivy and lifted her as easily as if she were a babe.

As she was curled into the creature's chest, Ivy saw Jack being scooped up, his mouth also covered securely.

There was no chance of escaping, not against two of them, not with her sword out of . . . *where is my sword?* She'd had a hand curled round the hilt when she fell asleep. She flexed her hand, moving her arm the slight bit she could.

"Stay still, princess, we don't want Jorge or the rodent to hear," the Glaistig whispered, her breath warm on Ivy's face.

Then, they were moving, but it was the queerest sense—as if time were stilling, as if the air itself were freezing around them. Ivy'd traveled in so many different ways, but none had felt so odd. The very peculiarity of the process made her stay as motionless as she could. Though she'd never heard of the Glaistigs having time-shifting skills, she couldn't think of any other way to explain the reversal of vibrations.

Almost as abruptly as they begun moving it was over. Ivy felt her feet hit solid ground as the Glaistig lowered her and uncovered her mouth. "Jack Merry?"

"I'm here." Jack's voice echoed. "Though I'm not sure where *here* is. Are you hurt?"

"No." Ivy could see shadows moving in the dim room, darknesses within the dark. The air was cold and damp, but in the distance, she heard water trickling over rocks. "We're with the Glaistigs, Jack. And I mean truly *with* them. They're in the room."

Several sets of hooves clopped in the stillness.

Ivy added, "Surrounding us, I believe."

"Do you have your sword?"

She squatted down and felt around on the slick floor, damp with what she hoped was water-sludge or cave-moss, not something worse. "No."

"And do you think you'll need it, little princess?" The voice was right beside her. "Do you think that wielding your sword is necessary here?"

Ivy shivered, but she straightened her back and called out, "Can you give me a little light, Jack Merry?"

"Umm . . . sure." Jack's voice was as unsteady as she felt. "The princess glanced upwards, and there on the ceiling was a glimmering ball of light, shining well enough to illuminate the . . . chamber."

As he spoke, the light blinked on and grew bright enough that Ivy could see a full score of Glaistigs grinning and watching them. They were spread out in a wide oval around Ivy and Jack, making it obvious that the only way out was through the well-armed women.

Ivy crossed the chamber--a high-ceilinged cave--and stood beside Jack. Taking a deep breath, she started to read the oghams carved on each flank until she found the elder. Battling her would be the best choice; defeat the matriarch and the others would stand down.

Now, let's see if Jack can fetch my sword from where ever they've hidden it.

"There's one more thing I need, Jack."

"Jonquil?" Calder stood beside her. His hand didn't rest on his weapon belt, but he scanned the area as alertly as if the Bog Mother were still with them.

"Umm?" Jonquil watched her sister splash around with Hagan, far more at ease than she'd been in a long while.

"Are you staying?" The young guard's posture didn't change. "Should I tell them to fix your rooms . . ."

Sighing, Jonquil glanced up at him. He was one of the youngest guards, far more cautious than Hagan and his year-mates. "Not yet, Calder. Not yet." Jonquil glanced back at the water.

There was a telltale smirk on Hagan's face as Daisy's voice carried over the swamp, "I might have missed you some too. But that doesn't mean . . ."

Hagan whooped and said, "But if I were to ask to come along with you . . ."

Daisy shushed him, their voices dropping lower.

On the bank, Calder squatted down, "If Grandmother Nogs

allows it, he'd travel with you. *Many* of us would." He lowered his voice further, adding, "It's a just thing you're trying."

Jonquil nodded. "And if I wanted to leave Daisy and Matty here? If I asked you to keep them here? What then?"

Calder shook his head. "Hagan . . . he'd try if you wanted him to keep her here. You know how he feels. *Everybody* knows he'd rather be with Daisy, but he'd rather we go with you than to stay here. As to Matty . . . we'd try." He gestured to the thicket where a growing number of guardsmen hovered. "But it's not keeping your sisters here that we're offering. We will if that's our only way of helping you, but we're asking to come. Get Grandmother Nogs' blessing."

Looking at their faces, eager and believing in her, Jonquil thought of Grandmother Nogs' demand the last time she'd visited: no discussion of help unless she promised to take over as Bog Mother. It wasn't a plan she liked, but Daisy and Matty would be happy.

Jonquil stood up and nodded. "I'll speak to her."

JACK LOOKED AT THE GOAT-FOOTED WOMEN, RECOGNIZING several of them from outside the inn at Pwca Vale. Water dripped from stalactites above them, dripping into puddles on the floor. Ivy had moved to stand beside him and was steadily staring at the strange symbols that were marked on exposed skin of the women's legs.

Perhaps that's the language here?

He quickly glanced at the markings too, but they didn't look the letters he'd learned.

One of the women moved closer. "Are you seeking something, little mortal?"

"Answers." Jack smiled as he caught her gaze. "I'm not so sure where we are, why we're here . . ."

Ivy brushed his hand with hers, but he wasn't sure if she was urging him to be quiet or keep talking.

"We thought it best to talk here." The woman's smile vanished as quickly as it had arrived. "Jorge's no friend of ours. He'd not let us speak with you earlier, so we waited until the rodent girl scampered off."

"Fiona left?" Ivy's surprise was apparently enough for her to forget her own fears for a moment. "I thought she was guarding our rest."

"So did Jorge." The woman scowled. "We were watching though."

Several women stamped their feet in the silence that followed the soft-spoken reply. Their footsteps thundered in the cave until one of the women spoke. "Princess. I remember you far better than I'm sure you remember me. You were not yet walking when I last came to the Queen's home."

She was more heavily armed than the others with a pair of swords crossed over her back, hilts jutting above her shoulders like the tips of wings. At least three shorter blades were fastened to her belt. But it was the symbols that startled Jack as he watched her move forward. Her entire leg seemed covered in them.

"Do you mean us harm, Matriarch Sezja?" Ivy stepped in front of Jack. Even without a weapon, she moved between him and what might be a threat. "Should I find a way to defend myself?"

Sezja shook her head. "No. I meant to save you from whomever the rodent girl went to fetch. She'd spent long hours with your sister when the Royal Deceiver was here."

The others stamped again, ane Jack was beginning to suspect was their way to say they agreed.

"Your mortal wouldn't survive long without your help." She paused to survey them again, lifting an eyebrow as she did so, seeming to find them somehow lacking. "I thought it best to bring you to my home first. From here, you can take him back aboveground."

Jack suspected he shouldn't interrupt, but he did. "I'm not going aboveground just yet. I'm staying with Ivy."

Ilanya snorted. Several others exchanged glances.

As if she hadn't heard, Ivy said, in a rather emotion-less voice, "Why would he leave, Matriarch? Jack Merry can set things to right. Mother will see . . ."

An unmistakable look of weariness crossed Sezja's face. Her eyes drooped closed for a moment before she answered. "What you do is noble, child. It's not worth the mortal's life though. It's not what his parents would want, not what you should want after all this time watching out for him."

"My parents?" Jack gaped at her.

Did she know what happened to them? His mouth felt dry, as if he hadn't had a drink in days. *Perhaps they survived.*

"What do you know about my parents?"

Ivy looked over her shoulder at him and squeezed his hand. "Nothing, Jack. The matriarch obviously seeks to trick us." Then, she whispered, "Could you summon my sword now?"

He looked past her to Sezja.

Jack thought he'd stopped hoping that his parents would return to him some day. He thought, after all this time, he had accepted their absence. *Especially now, after what Ivy said about that night.* Obviously, he was wrong.

Angry that the Glaistig tried to toy with his feelings, he looked away from her. Then, he closed his eyes and imagined Ivy's sword. He thought of the vines etched in the blade, the heavy weight of it in Ivy's hand. "The princess opened her hand and as she did so her sword returned to her. Its hilt in her hand as it should be."

Ivy curled her hand around it and nudged him behind her. "He's staying with me, and we need to be on our way, so let's talk about you moving out of our way."

"I'LL COME WITH YOU IF YOU'RE GOING." HAGAN SMILED AT her, as if his foolish grin would take away the seriousness of what he suggested. "Just say the word."

"You know that isn't my choice, Hagan. Grandmother Nogs makes the decisions." Daisy watched him scan the bank before they headed back towards the camp. For all his foolishness, he was a good guard.

"You could ask her . . . tell her how lost you are without protection. How you miss me." He slipped an arm around her shoulders and pulled her closer. With his free hand he signaled the sentry that stepped forward as they neared the border of the village. "You are, right? Lost without me?"

Daisy thought about crossing the tunnel—the Twitches screeching, Jack's wound from saving her and her sisters, the terrible tiredness in Ivy's voice. She shivered. "I don't think there's much chance of succeeding. The Hunt rides for the slightest thing these days. The Queen Mother either has no grasp on the folk's suffering or no longer cares. Just getting this far has been awful."

Hagan stopped and stared at her, serious and not hiding it for a change. "So, stay here. Instead of me going, you stay."

Daisy looked at him. She'd known Hagan longer than she'd known most anyone in the realm. Most of the Bollynoggins had barely tolerated her and her sisters when they first came to stay with Grandmother Nogs, but even then, Hagan had been different. He'd taught her how to find her way over the swamp trails. He taught her how to defend herself—against swamp rats and against his rough and tumble brothers.

"Daisy?" He hugged her to him. "You're scaring me."

"You need to stay here." She rested her head on his chest and fought the urge to weep as she told him, "If you come . . . the Queen will believe Grandmother Nogs is treasonous. In an instant she could boil the swamp, dry it up. There's no way to keep everyone here safe . . . Not to mention the Hunt or letting the Durgs out of the castle."

"And if you go?"

"If she goes, it's her choice alone." Jonquil stepped from the thicket with as little sound as the Bog Mother. "She can stay here. You can make her stay if you have it in you, Hagan. Matty too."

"He can keep me here? Really?" Daisy stepped back from Hagan and glared at her sister. "And how would he do that?"

She felt Hagan tense.

"By explaining how much safer you'd be here," he muttered.

Daisy ignored him, her temper finally simmering. She'd put up with enough from her sisters. "What happened to the comforting things you told Clematis? What about your refusal to go to Uncle Con's and wait it out?"

Jonquil shrugged.

Daisy started walking towards her sister. "If Ivy's successful . . ."

"And if she's not?" Grandmother Nogs' voice interrupted as she stepped into view. "Do you truly think the Queen's power can be undone by Ivy's mortal? Jonquil is right about this, Daisy: it's wiser for you and Matty to stay here." She glanced quickly at Jonquil, scowling. "It'd be wiser still for Jonquil to stay, but she's been bucking for a rebellion too long now for me to think she'd stay."

"What are you talking about?" Daisy sputtered.

Bucking for rebellion?

She looked from the Bog Mother to Clematis, who stood beside her—longbow in hand. Clematis was watching Jonquil, not looking at all shocked by the sheer ridiculousness of the Bog Mother's comment.

"I'll do it." Jonquil turned around, her expression terrifyingly desperate. "I'll mind the swamp, give up my wings, whatever you'll have of me." She stepped up to the Bog Mother and knelt on the ground before her. Peering up at Grandmother Nogs, she said, "Help us do this and afterwards I'll do whatever you'll have of me. I'll take care of the boys . . . better now than I could've before. Jack Merry gave me a healing touch. I'll care for all of them. You can retire. Stay here. Go. Whatever you want."

For several minutes, the only sounds were the calls of wiskins and a few frogs as they meandered through the hidden passage-ways on the bank. Daisy looked away from Jonquil to Clematis, to Hagan, to the Bollynoggins and the bodyguards. They all looked as shocked as she felt. Only Grandmother Nogs looked nonplussed by Jonquil's outburst.

Jonquil hadn't moved. She stayed, kneeling on the ground.

Grandmother Nogs sighed. "I can't, Jonquil. I can't send my boys there. I'll keep your sisters here and keep them safe, but that's all I can offer you." She reached out and laid her hand on Jonquil's cheek. "If you survive, you're welcome here. If you wanted to mind the swamp, I'd gladly accept it. I shouldn't have asked it of you, not like that at least. If you don't want it, just come back and stay with us."

Jonquil nodded, but the look on her face was awful to see. She looked broken and lost.

No one spoke. Clematis looked at her, looking almost as lost as Jonquil.

Daisy took a deep breath and said, "I'd rather go."

Clematis nodded. "Me, too."

Jonquil turned to face her, and Daisy held out a hand to help her to her feet. Clematis came to stand on the other side of Jonquil. She brushed a hand over Jonquil's tear-wet cheek.

"But someone has a lot of explaining to do . . ." Daisy added with a scowl at Jonquil. Her motherly sister was a revolutionary.

Chapter 12: In which they may have an ally

꧁꧂

Ivy held her sword at ready and spread her feet a little for better balance. The Glaistigs were some of the finest fighters in the realm. When she was a girl, she and Clematis used to make up tales of what would happen if the Glaistigs battled the Red-Caps or stood against the Hunt. Clematis always argued that the Red-Caps would win, while Ivy'd argued for the Glaistigs. Now, as she looked at them surrounding her, she hoped she'd been wrong about their being undefeatable.

"Do you think that's wise, Princess Lillian?" Sezja's voice had as much humor as warning in it.

"I'm not seeing too many choices, Matriarch Sezja." Ivy glanced at the Glaistigs. Not a one had moved. Several of the young ones had their hands on dark hilts, but the blades were still safely sheathed. "I'm not going to stay here, and going back above-ground isn't a choice."

Ivy glanced at Jack. "Take a look around. Picture it, Jack." She tore her gaze from his and looked pointedly at the stalactites and then back at him. They'd make a good weapon or, at the very least, a barricade. "I'm not sure how many I can fight."

Ilanya—one of the younger ones–spoke up, "We're not your

enemies. We carried you here in our arms, risked our safety for you."

Though the younger Glaistig hadn't asked permission, Sezja was letting her speak.

Ignoring Ilanya, Ivy took a deep breath and concentrated on keeping as many of the Glaistigs in sight as she could. She turned slightly from side-to-side as she waited, trying to see those that stood on each side as well as those in front of her. As to those behind them--listening for movement was the best she could do.

For now, at least.

The chances of getting out of the cave unharmed weren't good.

Ilanya spoke again. "Do you think we'd have rescued you only to harm you?"

"Perhaps." Then, for a moment, Ivy wavered.

Would they've done so?

She knew so little of the Glaistigs; they'd kept to themselves for as long as she could recall.

Why did they rescue us? Were we even in danger?

She was tired. Those few hours of rest had done little to offset the exhaustion of emotional upheaval and physical exertion. They had one day left to face the Queen, one day to try and change the realm. Three days was all Jack could have here, longer than that and too much time would have passed above-ground. That had been the rule back when mortals were allowed in the realm, and Ivy truly hoped to adhere to it. If they caused too much of a stir aboveground, there'd be a whole new set of troubles to answer for.

"So, what *do* you want?" Jack stepped up and gripped her arm lightly, stilling her.

She felt her body tense. *Find an answer, Jack Merry,* Ivy silently willed. *Please.*

But no one answered. The women just turned to Sezja.

Sezja remained silent for several heartbeats. Then, finally, the

Matriarch said, "We want peace, mortal. Peace for the Queen, peace for the realm, but there are those that would be a terror to the realm if you are injured. We cannot allow that if we could stop it."

"Who?" He sounded lost when he asked.

Ivy knew he was thinking about Sezja's earlier reference to his parents. Briefly, she wondered if the Glaistigs did know something.

Sezja shook her head. "It's not ours to answer, and the Princess knows not. There are forces that aren't as mighty as the Queen, but still are forces to fear. If we send you back, the realm stays as it is, but if you are wounded . . ." She shrugged. "It is not my wish to set that into motion."

Ivy caught the Matriarch's look of pain.

Maybe she was sincere.

Ivy couldn't tell with the Glaistigs. "If he goes back, there's nothing to keep us from returning, but it'd be more difficult to do so . . . more dangerous. If you truly want to keep him safe, sending him above-ground isn't the way."

Ilanya bowed to the Matriarch before suggesting, "If we spoke to them, those forces, told them that we'd tried . . . that the choice was not within our ability to sway."

"Would you do that, mortal? Come back here?" Sezja folded her hands together and pursed her lips.

"I would." Jack's voice didn't waver. "I gave my word to Ivy. I've seen the poisonous slime in the water, the fear in creatures' eyes. If you send us back, we'll just keep trying."

Ivy was sure Jack was as exhausted as she was, but he spoke as cleverly as he'd done with the Red-Caps and with the hound.

Maybe we can leave without bloodshed.

Again, the silence dragged on.

"Well, then, I suppose we should find you pallets so you can rest a bit. You'll need your energy if you're to have any chance at all." Sezja sighed and motioned for the Glaistigs to disperse. "We shall have to hope that our explanation is greeted with tolerance."

"If I may . . ." Ilanya murmured, stepped forward again. "Perhaps we could assist them. Assure that they are kept safe. Mightn't that assuage the fears of the concerned parties?"

"A wise answer." Sezja flicked her braid back over her shoulder where it drooped between those two jutting hilts. "We shall meet them at the Queen's palace. First, we must speak to those concerned parties. I'll make ready to address that matter. Ilanya, find them food and pallets."

And with that, Sezja departed.

Ilanya motioned to another dark passageway. "There are quiet rooms back here. Rest a while, then I'll take you to the path so you can rejoin the Ellyllon."

Jack started, staring at the grinning Glaistig. "How did you know?"

Ilanya laughed, and it was not a soothing sound at all. "Word of their progress was brought to Matriarch Sezja before we met. We'll catch them at the ravine."

Ivy began to wonder what force could frighten the Glaistigs.

Few things are worse than they are, if even the tamest rumours were true.

They slid through a narrow passage into another cavern, Ivy saw the pallets and thick furs on the floor, and she stopped wondering about everything. She all but collapsed onto the crude bed. Her tension slipped away and, with it, consciousness.

Two egrets stood ready. Hagan, Calder, and a third guard waited on the first egret. The second one had six more fully armed guards.

"We'll send them right back," Jonquil murmured to Grandmother Nogs. She didn't beg, didn't ask the Bog Mother to re-consider. She wanted to, but she didn't.

The Bog Mother nodded. "I know."

She hugged all three of them and then turned to stare out at the wiskins peeking their still-wet faces out from among the dense swamp grass.

As they climbed aboard the egret to leave the swamp, Clematis was uncharacteristically quiet. Once they lifted off, she waved at Grandmother Nogs; then she just stared over the swamp.

Jonquil didn't feel much more cheerful than Clematis looked. It was a far cry from the way she'd felt when they'd arrived.

What will we do now?

She closed her eyes to contain her tears of frustration.

Behind her, she heard Daisy still trying to explain her choice to Hagan. "Ivy and Jack are doing the right thing. I've been with her, looking out for her so long. I can't leave her . . ."

"It's the right choice. I just want to stay with you." His voice was rough, pleading. "Say the word."

Jonquil'd worked for so long at convincing Grandmother Nogs that she had been almost certain that the support would be there when the need arose. Jonquil wiped away her tears: they wouldn't help. Everyone wanted things to be *right* again, but convincing them to risk their own safety was a different matter altogether.

After the scores of meetings, I should've known better.

"Do you think they've passed Pwca Vale?" Hagan asked, voice somber. "Or should we stop?"

Jonquil looked down. There was no sign of the horse outside Jorge's inn. It might not be a guaranteed safe spot, but it was the best of the lot. Odds were that Ivy wouldn't have taken Jack to any of the other inns. "I suppose they got an earlier start."

Calder and the other guard stood back-to-back, eyes to the sky, bows held at ready—as if extra vigilance now would make up for the lack of back-up later.

She wondered if Ivy and Jack had run in to trouble at Pwca Vale. By now, half the realm surely knew of Ivy's breaking the *geas*. Word of change spread faster that fireworms in a dry field.

"Keep going." Daisy squeezed Hagan's arm. "If we don't see them, we'll wait at the far side of the ravine."

Hagan nodded, and they all resumed their silence.

§◆

JACK SAT ON THE FLOOR, EATING THE STRANGE BLUE MEAT THAT Ilanya had left for them. Across from him, Ivy slept in a nest of furs, either unaware of how damp the cave was or too tired to care.

He sat there, watching her sleep and listening to the steady chime of bells. He could hear them all the time now, like a song that never ends, but they were solid and deep as they tolled. If he wasn't so afraid of what that meant, he'd ask Ivy. If it were bad news, he'd rather neither of them knew.

Leaning back against the wall, he watched water trickle along a seam between long sheets of rock and pour through a crevice into a river somewhere beneath them. He couldn't see it, but he heard it—rushing away into some undoubtedly beautiful and terrifying corner of the realm.

Ivy mumbled in her sleep.

Briefly, he glanced at her; then he returned to watching that stream of water and listened to the tolling bells until his eyes grew heavier and drifted shut.

§◆

CLEMATIS WATCHED THE PATH. SHE'D GIVEN UP ON PRETENDING not to panic. It hadn't convinced anyone.

"Do you think they're injured?" Jonquil murmured from the

branch above her, sounding far less sure of herself since they'd left the bog.

"No." Clematis reached into the pile of food Daisy had dumped beside her earlier and plucked out a nut. "I just wish they'd get here."

"Are you angry with me?"

"Not really." Clematis picked up another nut and whacked the two together, splintering the shells so she could pick out the meat. "Think you should've told us though."

"I didn't want to upset Daisy."

Clematis snorted. "So that's why you didn't tell me?"

At first, Daisy didn't answer. Clematis could hear her get up and start pacing on the branch above. She cracked another pair of nuts and waited. It was a rare treat to be the sister who deserved the explanation rather than one who owed it.

"No. At first I didn't tell you because I was afraid of what you'd do." Jonquil was still pacing, her footsteps quick and steady. Every so often leaves would flutter by as Jonquil stomped or spun too suddenly.

"And?"

"And then I hadn't told you for so long it was a matter of admitting I'd kept a secret—and a big secret at that." Jonquil floated down to sit next to her. "You and Daisy always seem to think all I cared about was tending animals. How was I to say I wanted to change the realm?"

Clematis stared at her. Daisy was great for lectures and reminding everyone what the rules were, and Jonquil had always been the one to know what to say if things were uncomfortable. Finding herself in the position of needing to find the right words *for* Jonquil was a new experience. She took her sisters' hands and said, "Next time you decide to do something ridiculously brave, I'd rather hear about it from you than someone else."

"I will." Jonquil nodded and pulled a berry from the pile of food. She paused, fruit halfway to her mouth, and said softly, "Do you think Daisy's still angry?"

Grinning, Clematis pointed to the nest where Hagan and Daisy sat sharing their meal. "For now, she's distracted. Later, well, from now on really . . . you can count on her mentioning it when you irritate her. You'll get used to it."

§.

AS THEY WENT AROUND THE CORNER, JACK HALF EXPECTED THE ground to crumble away. When Ilanya said 'ravine' she forgot to mention how far down it went. Sheer rock walls dropped below them like they'd reached the edge of the world. A trail, little more than the width of the water-horse's steps, wrapped slowly down into that seemingly never-ending depth, and Jack wondered yet again at the sheer variety of the realm.

"We used to throw intruders off this ledge." Ilanya broke into his reverie, her voice soft with an almost nostalgic tone. "You could hear their screams echo through the gorge."

"Oh." Jack wasn't quite sure what the appropriate response was or if there was one.

"Sometimes when I was still little, we'd go above-ground and seek out the most horrible mortals we could find so we could toss them over." She made a little noise, like a purr almost.

"I see."

She laughed, a curiously beautiful sound considering the conversation. "Really, you should've seen it. We'd wait in the rivers, dragging them under until they stopped thrashing, then we'd bring them home and nurse them back to health. Once they were fit, we'd bring them to the ravine and *push*," she made a slight shoving gesture with her hand, "there they went, flailing and kicking."

"Ilanya?" Ivy interrupted.

"Umm?" The Glaistig was prancing along the narrow

passageway with as much grace as the Ellyllon had in flight. Her hooves were obviously far more suited to the uneven terrain than Jack or Ivy's feet.

Ivy was watching the ground at her feet as she walked. "I do believe that you're startling Jack just a bit."

Jack grimaced.

Ilanya looked at him, eyes wide. "Truly?"

"No harm." He forced a smile, feeling unreasonably embarrassed at his discomfort. She tormented mortals and regardless of how 'truly terrible' they were, it seemed wrong. But it seemed wrong to upset her too. "It's just different than how I'd do things, I think."

Ilanya snorted. "Mortals. There's no reasoning with you. We'd only take the awful ones, the ones deemed evil by human standards." She caught his gaze, as if willing him to understand. "It's not as if we'd take good ones, just like trimming a plant. *Pluck,* and off come the useless leaves."

"Ilanya?" Ivy interrupted, still not looking at the Glaistig or at him as she spoke, staring at the ever-deepened gorge instead. "Have your kind always been able to shift time?"

"As far as the folk know, we cannot do such a thing, Princess. Surely if we could, the Queen herself would know." Any trace of Ilanya's laughter was gone. Her lips were drawn in a tight line. Her hand flexed as if seeking something to grip. "If a generous queen before your own mother had allowed us such a skill as a boon . . . well, that would be in a time long since passed."

He felt it, that rising tension between them—almost as if it were a solid thing growing in the dusty air between them.

Ilanya stepped in front of them and stared until they were both watching her. Then she looked down into that deep gorge and casually kicked a rock over the edge with her hoof. "Having knowledge of such a secret could be dangerous. What the Queen knows, she can change. What she doesn't . . ." She shrugged.

"There's not much my herd would hesitate to do to keep such a secret—ˆ we had that skill."

Jack stepped forward, but neither Ivy nor Ilanya moved. Ivy was closer to the edge, putting him squarely between the two fey creatures.

Is it always like this? Moods here change as suddenly as the breeze.

He wasn't as alarmed as he'd been when they faced the hound, but he still felt as if something unpleasant squirmed in his belly, excited and afraid all at once.

But then Ivy smiled, ever-so-slightly. "One can always hope that such a skill would be used for the good of the realm."

"Indeed." Ilanya's entire posture relaxed; her grin returned. "If such a skill were truly ours, we'd only use it in dire circumstances—to protect our own or those we deemed necessary to the well-being of the realm."

And this isn't considered mad, he reminded himself. *This is normal.* He shook his head as they carefully would their way down the rim of the gorge.

"THEY'RE HERE!" DAISY LET OUT AN UNCHARACTERISTICALLY shrill noise. She couldn't help it: she'd been worried to the point of imagining the worst, horrible scenarios ranging from Jorge serving Jack up as a meal to the Huntsmen coming upon them as they slept. From there, she'd even started imagining less probable fates—staked out and bound by vine-gnarlers, held for ransom by free-ranging Durgs.

"They're here, but not alone," her sister added.

Jack and Ivy were slowly hiking down the last bit of trail, accompanied by—of all strange surprises—a grinning Glaistig. Aside from seeming inordinately slow, they appeared fine, but the Glaistigs were as likely to grin during trouble as not. Solicitous up until they skewer their victim, and often afterwards as well, that was their way.

Clematis nudged Jonquil, who'd started to drowse a bit. "Wake up."

"They don't look to be prisoners," Hagan said, nocking an arrow just the same. His attention was fixed on the approaching group. "Just say the word. It's not long enough to pierce her heart, but I can get an eye. Matty, you take her right eye; I'll take the left."

Jonquil had already risen to the air and was hovering by the branch where Hagan was standing at wait. "Daisy calls it—neither of you is to let loose unless she says to."

Surprisingly, Clematis and Hagan both grinned and nodded.

At least they were behaving. Daisy opened her mouth to ask Jonquil what she was doing.

Jonquil grabbed her hand and squeezed. "I'm going closer." Before Daisy could answer, Jonquil zipped off towards Jack and Ivy.

If we survive this, I'm going to get help looking out for them. Maybe Grandmother Nogs can offer some advice.

Sighing, Daisy said, "You heard her. Hold your position."

"WHAT?" JACK GLARED AT ILANYA.

She'd covered her mouth with her hand, trying to muffle her growing chortles.

Ivy put a restraining hand on his wrist. "Relax, Jack. Her kind has an odd habit of seeing humour where we mightn't." She pointed to the branches of a solitary tree where Clematis and one of the Bollynoggins had arrows trained on them, presumably intending to wound the Glaistig.

"Eyes or throat, little ones?" Ilanya called out, her voice echoing in the chasm.

"Eyes, I believe." Jonquil appeared up beside Ilanya's head, a surprisingly cruel smile on her tiny mouth. "Though I suspect they could try for the throat with the second volley."

Ilanya stared at Jonquil for several heartbeats. Then, quicker than a lizard capturing an insect, she snatched the Ellyll from the air. "And would you tell them to fire if I held you like such?"

"I would." Jonquil promptly sunk her teeth into Ilanya's hand, drawing blood.

As Ivy and Jack stood, mouths gaping, Ilanya released Jonquil. "Good for you, girl!"

"Do I understand that you mean them no harm, then?" Jonquil hovered just as close as she had before, seeming unfazed by her brief imprisonment in the Glaistig's hand.

"Today, at least." Ilanya winked, then turned to face Jack and Ivy. "May you find the path less terrible than I fear."

And she was gone, galloping up the steep path at a remarkable speed.

"Will we see you there?" Ivy called out.

Ilanya paused, stirring a cloud of dirt and dust as she spun on one hoof to look down at them. "With strange surprises in tow should all go as planned."

Ivy waved once, and then turned to Jack. "That went rather well, don't you think?"

With Jonquil perched on his shoulder, Jack stood, shaking his head again.

Ivy smiled at him and took his hand. "We are unharmed, and may have found an ally."

"You're a strange girl," he said, squeezing her hand. "But I think I like you."

"Oh . . . " Ivy tilted her head and watched him. "I thought you liked me before. Did you just decide?"

He laughed then, harder than she'd ever seen him in all the times she watched him.

"What?" She repeated it several times, but he just laughed and shook his head.

Mortals were an odd bunch.

She looked at Jonquil: the Ellyll shrugged.

Then Jack started to run down the path, towards the other Ellyllon, pulling her with him.

Chapter 13: In which they come to a moat

❦

A short while after they were reunited, they set off again, filling one another in on the events that had transpired.

"So, Grandmother Nogs will not help?" Ivy fought a sigh at the unexpected bad news. She had hoped that the Bollynoggins had spirited the Ellyllon away because the Bog Mother was interested in offering aid.

"The Glaistigs are far fiercer." Clematis looked a bit worn, but her smile was still in place. She'd been as bad as Daisy, hovering around them and asking questions about meals and rests. "If we're only to get one of the two, I'd rather it be the more vicious of the two."

She winked at Daisy. "No offense to Hagan."

"None taken." Daisy grinned at her sister.

Obviously, the trip to the bog had been good for them.

Jonquil landed on Ivy's shoulder. ""I'm not even sure we should continue. I had hoped . . . I thought if you brought the mortal, Jack, if you brought him . . . I thought the folk who'd met and talked would join us."

Ivy nodded. She'd had much the same hope: that somewhere along the way help would appear.

"We're on our own, and I'm not sure what we can actually do. I don't have a plan." Jonquil wrapped her hand in Ivy's hair as she spoke. "Do you?"

"I just know that we need to get in to see the Queen, but a plan? No. Not yet." Ivy kept on the path that would lead to her mother. With all the obstacles they'd encountered, they'd had no time to sit and devise a plan to approach the palace, and it was beginning to look like they'd need one. "But we will." She turned her head to look at the worried Ellyll. "You were right. Don't doubt yourself now."

This time, Jonquil nodded.

JACK TRIED NOT TO THINK ABOUT THEIR BLEAK ODDS; THEY were finding more trouble at every step. *We'll figure it out. We've done pretty well so far.* "Do you think we can enter the palace through the front? Is there a back door or something?"

They stopped. They were at the edge of a strangely appealing moat. The silvery water shimmered, as if something wonderful were waiting just below the surface.

"No." Ivy didn't say more though, turning her attention to the water-horse.

It obviously wasn't an intended stop: Ivy's water-horse refused to take them any nearer to it, snorting in apparent irritation as Ivy tried to urge him forward.

"Come now." She ran her hand over his great neck. "It's water, dear. Surely, you're not refusing to cross water."

"Perhaps, he's hungry . . ." Daisy dove into Ivy's satchel while Jonquil employed Clematis to help her inspect the horse's hooves.

Jack slipped to the ground, stepping closer to that liquid silver. It was quite a way down, but he knew how to swim. The Ellyllon could simply fly across. He started to turn to suggest just that to Ivy when he heard the most beautiful voice, like it was wrought of pure wonder, resonant and strong. Yet no sooner than he'd thought this, he was certain the creature that would carry that voice must surely be fragile. He could think of no reason that this would be true, but he was as certain of it as he was of his own name.

He heard the others tending the horse, but they didn't matter. Not now. He lay down on his belly, his hand dangling over the edge, to reach the gentle creature with that pure voice.

"Just a wee bit closer, darling." Her voice was only for him; none of the others were important.

Jack edged closer. His ankle tangled in ground vines, and he kicked. Once free, he could go over.

Almost there. . .

He saw her then, hair like silver rivulets streaming to her ankles, turning into drops of water as it touched the surface of the moat. She looked every bit like a mother should—like those other mothers that were never his. Her eyes shined with pride. He was certain that's what it was, pride that he'd tried to find her.
. .

Yes, that wretched Ivy lies, telling him he was some worthless mortal when really, he was her son.

Jack nodded, trying desperately to kick his ankle free, to reach her.

His mother, for real and true, and she'd take him to meet his father and his brother. In just a moment, all he had to do was come closer.

"Just take my hand, sweetling." She rose out of the water, towering like mighty waterfall, her arms open to embrace him.

But then Ivy was there, gripping his legs, trying to stop him from reaching his home. "Jack! You mustn't listen."

Ivy was not his friend. She'd use him, destroy him, and leave him alone again in that mortal realm. It was so cold there, so lonely.

Keeping his gaze fastened on his mother, his beautiful mother, he kicked at Ivy.

"Come to me." His mother wept, letting loose a wail that

made his lungs tighten. "You're so close, my sweetling. I've waited for you, suffered so long."

Jack dug his hands into the soil, trying to pull himself free of Ivy's hateful grasp. His fingers bled and burned.

It was nothing compared to his mother's pain.

Ivy clung to his leg like a leech.

Below his mother's cries, Jack heard Ivy calling her minions. "Hurry, Jonquil!"

Then, Jonquil was there, brushing thistle-coated fingers on his ears.

He squirmed, trying to evade her.

He couldn't let go of the soil or Ivy would be able to drag him away from his mother's embrace. He was too close to let that happen.

"Listen, Jack Merry. Listen and be well." Jonquil slid her hand over his forehead.

And Jack truly heard her, the thing that had been calling him. Her voice was a cacophony of screams, like the voices of drowning men and wailing mothers. It was the sound of water gargling in lungs, filling them until there was no room for precious air.

He scuttled backwards like a crab, frantic and awkward.

"Well, then, the first battle goes to you, Princess." The creature sunk into the oily water of the moat until only her head remained above the slick surface as if it were floating there.

"Stay behind me, Jack." Ivy was breathing as if she'd been running a great distance under the midday sun. "Please, move back."

Jack obeyed without hesitation.

"Until later, sweetling." The creature laughed, and Jack felt as if the fingers of long-dead bodies squirmed in his stomach.

🦂

"WHAT WAS THAT?" JACK TREMBLED, LEANING HEAVILY ON THE flank of the water-horse.

"That, Jack Merry, is an abomination." She kept herself between Jack and the moat. If she'd known that her mother or Ada had brought out a Coira, she'd never have let Jack close in the first place. "She can read what you've most recently thought, what you want so desperately, twisting it, making a glamour for herself so as to tempt you."

Clematis hovered near. "It only works on menfolks."

". . . that means that Ada expected you to come here, Jack." Jonquil looked at him intently, fluttering just in front of his face. She bowed her head then, sounding worn. "I've no idea how to pass her."

"Let's back away from her grasp while we figure a plan." Ivy steered Jack in front of her, trying to quash the image of him fighting to reach the Coira, to get where she could drown him. "Jack cannot change the Coira. He tried on one of the hounds, but the essential nature of a thing can't be altered."

Daisy wrestled open Ivy's satchel.

"It can. My nature was changed with his gift." Jonquil smiled as she went over to help her sister.

Without prompting, Daisy began passing out their meal. Fortunately, by Ivy's way of thinking at least, she had no way to find any more Drizzle Soup.

"Because you wanted it?" Jack rubbed his eyes. "That was part of it, right?"

"I did," Jonquil said as she brushed Jack's forehead again, unobtrusively.

Ivy knew she was trying to assure herself that he was well.

"And Ivy's stronger, for the same reason, I'd suppose," Jonquil added.

"But the Coira probably doesn't want to change." Jack stared towards the moat and shivered. "And if she claimed she did, there's no way to tell if it's a trick."

"So what can he change if not her nature?" Ivy wondered aloud. "Something small if we can think of it." She squeezed Jack's arm. "You get horribly tired after doing this, worse when you do bigger things."

They ate their snacks as they pondered.

All the while Ivy kept alert. Her sword might not be of use against the Coira's watery-form, but if she had to bop him on the noggin to restrain Jack bodily, that was still an option of sorts.

❦

JONQUIL HOPED THAT THEY HADN'T COME QUITE THIS FAR ONLY to be rebuffed at the gate. "What do we know about the Coira?"

"She's water fey, like the Glaistigs are if they go above-ground." Daisy spoke between trips to pile more food on everyone's plate.

"She can't go above-ground, though," Clematis added.

"Why?" Jack reached out and gently wrapped his hand around Daisy. Without a word, he plopped her beside his pile of food and shoved a piece of fruit towards her.

When he glanced at Clematis, waiting for her answer, Daisy started to flutter off.

Clematis popped a ridiculously large berry in her mouth, puffing her cheeks out like squirrel. "Mrm Mrffer."

"What?" Jack and Ivy stared at her.

Exactly! Jonquil thought. She grinned at Daisy. They'd get Jack past the Coira just fine.

Clematis swallowed and repeated, "Warm water. A Coira needs warm water."

Daisy hovered above the plate, leaving the fruit untouched, smiling proudly at Clematis.

Jack's shoulders lowered as the tension seeped away. "Then we'll take away her warm water."

"First, you must eat." Ivy pushed Daisy back to the fruit. "We *all* need to eat before we go on."

Jonquil looked around at them, finishing their food in silence.

Maybe we'll be fine after all, even without as much of the help I hoped we'd find.

"AND AS THE PRINCESS LOOKED AT IT, THE MOAT TURNED TO solid ice, thick as the coldest ice in the world, frozen clear through so not a single drop of water could move . . ." Jack shivered as Ivy led him onto the ice.

"Keep picturing, Jack Merry. Picture how solid it is, how the Coira cannot move." Ivy wished again that her horse had been willing to cross with them; she wasn't at all comfortable as they walked over the moat. "Stay focused. This close to Mother's throne, I've no way of knowing if she's apt to undo what you speak into being."

"Right. The ice is so very thick that everything in it is still, nothing moves, not a ripple." His feet weren't steady as they walked, slipping sideways on the smooth surface.

Tugging him as fast as she dared, Ivy hoped the Coira had no way of breaking free of Jack's will.

At Jack's insistence, the Ellyllon had already crossed and were waiting on the other side. The Coira had no sway over them, but she didn't need to trick them. All the water woman needed to do was to stop Jack: Ivy couldn't—wouldn't—slay her own mother. She wanted to save her word and her people, but to do that, she needed Jack's gift so they could *heal* her mother.

That meant crossing past every obstacle to reach the queen.

As they touched the almost-black grass at the other side of the moat, Ivy let go of Jack's hand. "We're across."

Jack opened his eyes, glancing back at the moat. As he did so, the ice shivered like it was erupting. A gash appeared in the surface.

"Move!" Clematis yelled.

From the gash, the Coira emerged like a moving ice-sculpture. She kept going, drawing the ice up higher and higher as if each water crystal was a part of her.

Ivy was tugging Jack's hand, but he couldn't move.

Stay with me. The Coira's voice wrapped around him like nothing else that could ever matter. *Please, sweetling, I'll never leave you again. Just stay. Stay with Mother.*

Shards of ice rained down like daggers.

Jack was dimly aware that Jonquil was trying to reach him, that Clematis was calling to him, that Daisy tried to keep her sisters out of harm's way.

They don't truly care. How could they *understand you?* Coira asked. *They aren't enough.*

Ivy's fingernails dug into Jack's palm, anchoring him in the present just long enough to see what was truly before him.

Jack suddenly smiled--the Ellyllon were fighting to reach him and a faery princess who'd risked her immortal life for him was trying to pull him to safety. It was enough.

The Coira's voice lost its charm, and she sunk back into the thawing moat.

Ivy led him further away from the moat.

His steps grew surer, confident that Ivy led him to safety. *Well, relatively speaking.*

Chapter 14: In which they breach the walls

❧❀❧

Of course, as they finally stood in front of the outer walls to the Queen's palace, Jack Merry suspected that no one was thinking that all would be well. He surely wasn't. The outer walls were covered with the tangled vines of a monstrous plant, its tentacles lashing the air. As Jack watched a bird flew too close to a writhing tentacle. Tiny teeth on the vine wrapped around the bird as other vines lashed around, waiting to snatch up the bits of feather and other things that fell.

"I see it, Jack," Ivy said calmly. "That's not usually there. My mother must be expecting us."

The Ellyllon buzzed about, murmuring amongst themselves.

Jack glanced at Ivy. "I could try to change it . . ."

"No. We've no time to rest after this, and once we're inside, things are sure to be worse. My sister Ada will have warned the Durgs and who knows what else to keep us from the queen." Ivy brushed her hair back, twisted it into some sort of towering knot, and fastened it with a strip of cord. Her leady wings flapped once, twice, and then stilled against her skin Then, she hefted her sword and said in forced cheer, "'This is no different than trimming a hedge."

Jack stared at it. Nothing remained of the bird, and the tentacles were flailing about again.

"There must be something I can do."

"Indeed, there is." She offered a wry smile. "If I'm terribly cut up, try to get me out so Jonquil can mend me. If not, take advantage of the vine's distraction and keep going."

Jack was aghast. "I can't leave you."

"If I fall, you must still go forward, Jack. You are the only one who can heal my mother," Ivy insisted. "She wants to be well. I'm certain of it, and if I'm right, you can save her, change her."

"But—"

"My job was to get you here, Jack," Ivy said firmly. "You must heal the queen."

Jonquil nodded. "We'll do what needs done to get him there, Ivy. Clear the path."

Daisy stayed silent, but Jack saw her nod briefly, too.

#

Ivy lifted her sword and began hacking at the vines. *At least they're not alive.* Thick tentacles landed alongside her with heavy thumps. *How can anyone look at a corruption of a thing's nature and not realize Mother needs help?*

As Ivy spun and ducked, she kept swinging, severing toothy plants and trying to prevent the slashing vines from cutting her. For the most part, she was succeeding. One tiny tendril had caught her hair and ripped a good handful out at the roots. Her wings had scrapes. Her already-dirty tunic was now ripped in countless places. Her arms grew heavy.

Even though she didn't speak of it, Mother knew that the folk met in secret, met and plotted.

Ivy looked at the towering length of the vine: it reached up beyond where even the strongest plants in the realm could reach, touching that false sky, almost pushing through it to the world above-ground.

If Jack couldn't help her, it'd be a matter of time until the folk turned against her mother. The Queen might not be a good *mother, but once she had been a tolerable mother. Before.*

Ivy paused, ignoring the lashing vines striking her and wrapping around her ankles. She forced her way deeper and deeper into the plant. Tendrils grabbed her, biting with tiny plant teeth and trying to stop her. Her tunic was tearing, and her skin stung from small bites. Larger tentacles could not reach her without tangling themselves.

Finally, she found the central stalk and took aim.

Ada would be a horrible Queen. If my sister were even a passable choice as a regent, the folk would have assassinated the Queen by now. They have no love for her anymore. All that stops them is that Princess Ada is worse.

With every bit of anger she could harness, Ivy swung at that central stalk of the vine, cutting deep into it.

This will work. Ada will not take the throne.

Ivy tugged the sword out of the meat of the vine. Green gelatinous slime clung to the blade. Once more she stabbed. This time the entire thing trembled, rapidly striking her over and over, tugging her ankle, trying to pull her away.

It will *work.*

One last time, she sliced the vine, severing it clear through. The entire plant collapsed on top of her, burying her under thick tentacles. Then, everything went dark, and Ivy let herself stay still. Until they pulled her out of the remains, Ivy could give in to her fears. No one would need to know how scared she was right now, how terrifying it was that she'd be wrong, how awful it would be if her mother couldn't be saved.

"Ivy!" Jack's voice sounded frantic. "Ivy! Where are you? Where is she? Is she . . I saw her fall."

The Ellyllon would be no help moving the heavy vine. Ivy's moment of admitting fear was already ended. Heroes didn't get time to be afraid.

"I'm here, Jack." She sighed and started pushing the vines

away. There'd be time for fear and hiding later, or there'd be no
need for any of it. "It's fine, Jack. I'm fine."

And she slid her blade through another nest of tentacles on
top of her, clearing a bit of space so she could move.

Jack pulled vines away, and she saw the scrapes and small cuts
where the plant's teeth had torn his flesh. Soon, his face was visible, brows drawn together and looking more afraid than she'd
seen him before.

"Give me your hand," he said.

She reached out, stretching toward him.

Jack helped lift her from the mass of plant pieces.

"See. Just like trimming a hedge," Ivy said.

#

While Jonquil tended to the slashes and scrapes covering Ivy,
Jack pretended he was calm. He'd listened to those tolling bells
drop slower and lower as she'd fallen under the monstrous plant.
That was when he'd panicked.

"Are you well enough to keep moving?" Jonquil's voice
betrayed mixed emotions, fear and worry and hope.

"Of course." Ivy nodded and tiny bits of plant matter shook
free of her hair, like a strange rain shower. "This is it. Mother will
be saved."

Jack sat on the ground beside her, not bothering to brush away
the shower of greenery that was falling around them. He saw the
tears in her wings, the scrapes on her skin, and he wanted to wait
while she recovered.

"We could rest," he said.

"Here? In the open?" Clematis asked incredulously.

"I'm fine to continue," Ivy stressed.

In front of them was the Queen's palace, Ivy's home. It wasn't
a faery palace in the way he'd imagined it, but then again, few
things here were at all what he might've imagined.

The area immediately around the palace door was a strange
structure of crumbling rock and what looked to be seashells.

Flowers sprouted from the sides at odd intervals, perhaps either as decorations or as some other defense. At spots it seemed that only pure chance kept the rocks from tumbling down. But, for no discernable reason, the further walls seemed fashioned out of a wholly different rock. It was almost glassy, black and slick like it was wet. He could see faint lines where bits of the rock had been chipped away, leaving jutting points that looked as sharp as Ivy's sword.

It was far from inviting.

Jack stayed on the ground, looking away from the crumbling doorway to study the ravaged plant.

Ivy did that.

She'd been like a sea squall given form, spinning and tearing down whatever stood in her path, but he'd seen her face in the middle of it. He'd glimpsed her expressions of determination and exhaustion, and several times had started towards her, only to be stopped by Clematis' stern admonishments. 'You'd be more trouble than help with this, Jack.' and 'She said for you to stay here.'

Each time, Jack had mumbled his acquiescence.

Now, he looked up at her, taking in the droop of her shoulders and the tremble in her hand. "Are you sure you're even able to go on?"

"I am," Ivy said with a visible straightening of her sagging shoulders. "And if I weren't, it wouldn't matter. We can't stay here, Jack. It's no safer sitting here than it is going forward."

He wanted to argue with her. He wanted to tell her they could turn back. Not because he was afraid for himself, though he supposed he should be, but because in that moment all he could think about was how tired she looked.

But going back wouldn't help her fix her world, and somewhere along their travels, that had become important to him. Or maybe Ivy was just important to him. He thought of the creatures he'd met along the way. They all waited and watched. Most weren't helping in the open—but who would dare commit trea-son? Who would face an angry, world-making queen? Only her daughter, a few tiny faeries, and one foolish boy.

He *had* to help her.

Jack stood up and stepped in front of her. "No more telling me to wait while you rush off."

Her eyes widened and a tiny furrow creased her brow.

"You said I shouldn't help because I get too tired, but . . ." He tugged her to her feet and lowered his voice so the others couldn't hear him. "You're exhausted, too. I can see it. So, either we go together, or we don't go."

"Fine." Ivy stared at him for a long minute and then walked off at a much faster pace than normal, as if to prove she was not tired at all.

Jack rolled his eyes and hurried after her.

With a slight thump, Daisy landed on his shoulder, gripped his ear, and murmured, "Well said!"

Then she darted away to join her sisters beside Ivy.

"I'm waiting, Jack Merry," Ivy called. She gripped the handle and motioned him forward with her free hand. "Try to keep up."

He bit his lip to keep from smiling at her irritation and sped up. Once he was at her side, he said, "I'm here."

Then, together they tugged open the door.

#

Not two steps into the vast white room, the Durgs were upon them. The rat-faced men swarmed from every nook and cranny of the chamber, clambering over crystalline sculptures, dropping from glittering chandeliers.

Clematis called out, "Behind you!"

Brandishing skull-tipped canes like rapiers, the Durgs quickly separated the group. Jonquil and Daisy were still with her, but Jack and Ivy were each on their own, surrounded by groups of Durgs.

Her back against a stark white wall, Ivy held her own, but in the middle of the chamber with only a fountain to offer any cover, Jack was utterly defenseless.

"Jack!" Ivy's screamed, and everything seem to slow.

Clematis turned in time to see Jack get bashed on head repeatedly by a contingent of Durgs. He was holding up his hands to protect his face, but blood seeped from at least three places. Falling, he braced himself on the edge of the fountain.

Durgs tramped through the water, unmindful of anything but attack. The clear water in the fountain's spray clouded with dirt and blood.

Clematis nocked another arrow and started picking off as many of the Durgs as she could. *Calm. No sense wasting the arrows by not aiming well enough.*

She was so focused on keeping her arm steady she didn't see the arrival of their unexpected back-up until Jonquil breathed, "The Bollynoggins are here." Her voice was almost reverent. "They came."

Clematis let loose another arrow and followed Jonquil's gaze to see Grandmother Nogs gesture to the archers.

Then, the room was full of arrows as the Bollynoggins fired on the Durgs, clearing a path toward Jack Merry.

Looking regal as she balanced on the back of a squirrel, Grandmother Nogs waved from the doorway. Her moss skirt and plump green legs were all but hidden under the fur of the squirrel's two tails, which were wrapped securely around her like a harness.

Clematis swooped to the left to avoid the blow of a skull-tipped cane.

"Grandmother," she said and nodded at her. Then, Clematis nocked another arrow and sighted down on a Durg whose aim was far too good to go unanswered.

With the arrival of unexpected back-up, and fierce back-up at that, the tide turned quickly, and in what seemed only a few moments, Ivy—with a bloodied, battered Jack Merry securely behind her—and Grandmother Nogs were both beside the Ellyllon.

Jonquil promptly flew to tend Jack's wounds.

The Bog Mother winked, and then turned to Jonquil. "I seem to recall you invited me to the fracas."

"I did." Jonquil looked up from a particularly bloody wound over Jack's eye. "Glad you could make it."

The Bollynoggins were like a moving wall around them, facing the Durgs and firing their arrows almost nonstop.

Ivy, towering above them, knocked back any Durgs that made it past the barrage of cactus arrows. The floor was littered with the tiny needles, their sharp tips and barbed sides piercing the Durgs when they fell.

Jonquil glanced down and added, "Not that I mind you coming, but why . . .?"

Without seeming to look, Grandmother Nogs spotted a Durg that had been creeping up on them. She bashed him with the spiked metal club she held in her right hand.

"Well, the boys were restless. Thought a trip would be good for them." Grandmother Nogs jabbed another rat-faced attacker. "And here's as good as somewhere else."

Behind them, a sculpture shattered under the blows of a group of Bollynoggins with clubs, raining crystal shards around them, making it difficult for the Durgs to cross the chamber.

A pair of egrets swooped down to extract the victorious Bollynoggins. They grabbed the vines that their brothers dangled and dangled from the birds as the egrets flew through the air.

Then, as one the Bollynoggins dropped from the vines, spreading out beside Grandmother Nogs.

Clematis smiled as their much larger group moved forward toward the long hallway that led to the Royal Chamber. "Glad you could join us."

"Couldn't let the boys go unsupervised." With a loud sigh, Grandmother Nogs swung the mace again, clobbering another

Durg. She grinned and added, "And I thought it'd be nice to crack a few skulls."

Now that Jack was steady again, Jonquil zipped off to a fallen Bollynoggin, and in moment had him back on his feet.

More Durgs vaulted from their hiding places.

A great egret with three Bollynoggins standing on its back dropped down. In tandem all three Bollynoggins on its back let loose their arrows, providing cover for Jonquil and the healed Bollynoggin.

"Help with the door, Jack." Ivy gestured with her sword. "Let's go."

Together, they tugged open the gleaming silver door, and the whole strange army streamed through.

Once the Bollynoggins were all through, Jack and Ivy slammed the door shut and slid the bolt, leaving the Durgs outside it.

"Persistent, aren't they?" Grandmother Nogs muttered, her gaze roaming over the Bollynoggins to assess the damage.

The Durgs were shoving against the door, pounding on it, and calling out rather awful threats that had to do with fires and meat spits.

"Ivy?" Jack said. "Look at the door for me."

After resting her head on his shoulder for a moment, she nodded.

Then Jack closed his eyes and said, "And the door was impervious, solid through and through to any that would harm Ivy."

Then, he tugged Ivy with him, and they followed the score of Bollynoggins that had taken point. "Come on."

Jonquil zipped back and forth and tended to whatever wounds she could, humming that silly song their mother used to hum. Hagan lectured Daisy on her lack of "a single piece of weaponry to protect herself."

Clematis grinned at all of it. *It was good to have help.*

Chapter 15: In which old kindnesses are remembered

⟡

They weren't but halfway down the hall when Ivy felt her throat constrict.

The Ellyllon and Bollynoggins rounded the corner, but Ivy froze, clutching Jack, pulling him to a stop beside her. Fear washed over her before she even saw them, but the time between fear and seeing them wasn't long enough to say anything to warn Jack.

From the depths of the palace, they came. Their faces were lost in a cloud of their own making. The Hunt rode toward them.

Skeletal hooves pounded over the marble floor as they came pouring into the room like a raging waterfall forced into a narrow channel. The hounds raced between those sharp hooves, a seething black mass with glowing eyes and bared teeth. Their experience with only one hound was difficult enough. The onslaught of innumerable hounds would be impossible to stand against.

This was it: the end.

It took everything she had to not flee.

"Ivy?" Jack stepped nearer to her, his breath warm in her hair. "You risked *that* to rescue me?"

She nodded; speaking was too hard with her heart thrumming inside her.

"And you said you were the reasonable one . . ."

She tore her gaze away from the approaching terror to glance at him: he was smiling.

He took her free hand in his. "You are truly amazing."

\#

Jack looked at them, this Hunt that Ivy's spoken of in such a shaky voice. They were as awful as she'd said. The closer they came, the more he felt the urge to run.

The dark horses were sheer muscle, seeming strong enough to run the span of the world without pause. With fathomless green eyes and huffing something foul-smelling with each breath, every aspect of the horses sent shivers over him.

The Hounds were like countless copies of the one they'd faced in the meadow--glowing red eyes and dripping slaver from impressive jaws--but the sheer number of them made it appear as if the ground moved. Like black waters in a flood, they flowed around the horses' bone-white hooves.

When he finally lifted his gaze to the riders, forcing himself to face them, his throat tightened. These were the creatures that controlled the terrifying beasts.

At first glance, the Huntsmen seemed like wraiths, some were covered by armor that absorbed the light, but as he looked steadily at them, he saw others with strange drawings on their skin, and others with sinewy muscles--honed, no doubt, by hefting the ferocious weapons they gripped.

They were all things of terror.

As Jack looked in their faces, he saw nothing: no emotion, no desire, nothing. If they'd looked angry or excited, anything, it would've been more comforting than that sheer emptiness in their expressions. It was like looking into an endless abyss.

If he weren't frozen by the fear crawling over his flesh, he'd run, run until his breath failed him. But he couldn't move.

He stared, mute, as they flowed toward him.

But--moments from trampling Ivy and him--the Hunt stopped. The Huntsmen stared down at him. The hounds and steeds stood as if frozen, only their strange eyes moved, tracking from Ivy to him and back again.

A Huntsman urged his steed forward, ahead of the rest. He stared from behind a mask of black spirals ending in curved metal tusks. It covered almost all of his face, exposing only the mouth and eyes. The Huntsman wasn't as tall as the others, seeming slight in form, but the others waited.

What horror hides behind that mask?

"Are you the mortal then?" The Huntsman spoke in a voice that was little more than a dry whisper. "The one that came unwelcome into the realm."

Jack nodded. He wanted to speak, but his lips wouldn't part.

Ivy's fingers dug into his hand, not crushing it, but far more fiercely than was comfortable.

"Shall we take you above-ground?" The Huntsman's horse moved forward more several paces.

No one else moved.

"No." Jack lifted his chin, trying to look into those empty eyes and failing. He repeated, "No. I stand with Ivy."

Ivy squeezed his hand tighter.

"If the Faery Queen orders, if her *will* is invoked, we have to do her biding. Come while we can take you above-ground and leave you there still breathing." The Huntsmen smiled in what may have been intended as a comforting look.

It wasn't.

Then, the masked hunter held out a hand, as Ivy had once done, and urged, "Come."

Jack shook his head again. "I can't. I gave my word." He looked at Ivy, silent beside him. "Her mother is ill. I promised to help."

The Huntsman lowered his hand.

"If the Faery Queen orders it, there's no mercy. We cannot disobey our queen." In that moment, the Huntsman looked almost pained, eyes widening, hand clenching the horse's dark mane. "If you come now . . ."

"I'm sorry." Jack didn't know why he was apologizing to this stranger. He tried a smile, but it felt more like a grimace. "Unless you stop me, I have to try . . . I don't want to make you do something you don't want to, but I have to try to help Ivy's mother."

"Princess." The Huntsman turned to Ivy, aiming that cold gaze at her. "You saved him once. Why would you do this?"

Ivy kept her firm grip on his hand. She shivered. She swallowed hard.

Finally, she said, "She is my mother. This is my home."

Before the Huntsman could reply, Jack added, in a slightly stronger voice, "It is my choice."

The Huntsman did not speak. None of them did. The animals stayed in their posture of barely contained movement, like a painting of a storm: it looks still, but somehow when you look closer, the stillness seems a trick.

Finally, the Huntsman nodded. "We have no order to stop you. Not yet." Through the mask, the hunter looked at Jack as if there were more to say more, then looked away to another rider in the front of the Hunt.

The second rider shook his head.

The Huntsman turned back to them.

"May you succeed before we are summoned, Jack Merry." The Huntsman nodded curtly to Ivy. "Princess. Go to your companions, and be swift. We will ride out until we are summoned. Perhaps it will allow you a few extra moments with our queen and the *other* one."

Then without any visible gesture or command, the terrifying steed joined the others and they were gone, taking away the disquieting energy they carried with them.

#

Ivy stared down the hallway, empty now. They'd faced the Hunt and were unscathed. *Never* had she heard of such a thing.

Jack turned to her. "What just happened?"

"That, Jack Merry, is a question I cannot answer." She shook her head. "On my vow, I have no idea. I've never thought they could be *kind.*"

"He seemed almost helpful." Jack flexed the hand she'd just released.

Small bruises were already forming on his knuckles where she'd gripped him too tightly.

"I've wounded you!" Ivy said.

"Come on." Jack took her hand in his again, briefly, to tug her forward; then, he released it. "I'm fine."

After several deep breaths, she nodded, and they rounded the corner. The Ellyllon and Bollynoggins all sitting on the floor, looking dazed. With them were the Glaistigs.

"The Hunt." The Bog Mother stared up at them--a bemused smile on her face. "You faced the Hunt, and you're not dead."

"No," Jack said, sounding surer now. "We did not face them. We only spoke to them. If they wanted to harm us or take us from here, we'd be done."

Ilanya winked at Jack. "Pretty astute for a mortal."

The Glaistigs all stomped and grinned. Their hooves clattered against the obsidian tile that led to the queen's throne room. They seemed eager and utterly unfazed by the Hunt's appearance.

But the Ellyllon and Bollynoggins looked awed, as if something astounding had happened.

And it had. No one spoke to the Hunt.

At least, Ivy had never heard of such a thing. She smiled at the Bog Mother. "Perhaps the Hunt realizes what we all realize--Jack can heal my mother."

No one argued; nor did they agree.

"Let's not waste the time they gave us," she added. "You stay behind us when we enter the chamber."

"We'll do our best to help you, Princess," Ilanya said, "but if the danger grows too great, we will take Jack Merry away from you if needs be. We have other bonds we must uphold. If the Hunt is called to end the mortal's life, we *must* act. Matriarch Sezja will see him home should such be necessary. "

"You'll stand against the Hunt?" Ivy stared at the throng of Glaistigs behind her. What Ilanya proposed was impossible. "No one stands against them."

"They may slaughter us all, but it'll be a fight worth seeing. It's been ages since we joined a truly bloody battle. The Red-Caps get all the fun these days." Ilanya licked her lips. Then, she winked. "Although, no one in the realm can do what we can, so in the midst of battle, if your mortal vanishes, it is not cause to worry . . . We will see him to Sezja's care . . . unless we are reduced to spatter on the floor."

Ilanya hadn't lost her cheerful expression as she added this last bit, nor had the Glaistigs and the Bollynoggins behind her.

"Open the door," the Bog Mother said softly. "She already knows we're here."

Ivy tried to shake away the awful thoughts crowding her mind: blood on the Faery Queen's floor, the tiny fey against the Hunt, the terrors that would follow. She swallowed hard. "Are you ready, Jack Merry?"

He nodded.

So, she opened the door to her mother's chamber and with the Bollynoggins and Glaistigs in tow, Ivy led Jack forward to meet her mother.

#

After all the obstacles in their path, Jack had expected the Faery Queen herself to be the height of nightmares. She wasn't.

She was a ghoulish woman, so painfully thin that her bones appeared close to breaking through her greyish-blue skin. The fur edged cloak draped over her shoulders and the crown of opalescent stones atop her head seemed to weigh her down, as if to shackle her to her plush throne. She didn't look like a thing of terror, pity perhaps, but not terror.

The room around her, however, invited fear. It was vast, fading to shadowed reaches, like peering into a great tunnel, no end in sight. What hid in those dark depths he didn't know, nor--in that moment--did he want to. It was not a room of comfort. The floor was cut of the same dark rock that was on the outside of the palace, slick and shining as if it were wet. Luminous white pillars rested at odd intervals in the room, supporting a star-scattered ceiling. He knew they weren't real stars, but the illusion was amazing.

"Mother." Looking graceful even in her tattered tunic, Ivy curtseyed.

Having never met royalty--other than Ivy--Jack had no idea how to greet a faery queen, so he knelt and bowed his head. Behind him, he heard the Glaistigs and Bollynoggins moving with rustles and clatters, and Jack suspected that they, too, bowed before the Faery Queen.

"You've broken the *geas*." The Faery Queen's voice hissed like a breeze escaping through a jagged hole. Obviously, she wasn't interested in wasting time on pleasantries.

"I have." Ivy stood. She held her hands loosely at her side, fingers not touching the silver hilt of her sword, but awfully close to it. "He can heal things, Mother. He could help you, help the realm."

Trusting that Ivy would warn him if he needed to act, Jack stayed kneeling while she spoke. He watched the haggard Faery Queen as she sat on the dais. She didn't look well enough to hurt them, but he supposed she had folk that would do that for her.

"I need no mortal's *help*." The Faery Queen coughed into a shimmering white cloth. When she pulled it away from her lips, blood stained it. "Ada helps me. She re-makes the fields so they are rife with promise, keeps the waters pure. Surely, you've seen them as you dragged this"--she lifted a bony hand, pointed at Jack --"through my realm."

Diaphanous layers of cobwebs behind the throne parted as Ada stepped forward. "I can assure you that they have, my queen." She took her mother's hand in hers and pressed a kiss to it. "Word has come that Ivy's mortal has changed the waters, undoubtedly without regards to the Royal Vision."

She sneered at them over the Faery Queen's head.

"Is this true, Ivy?" the Faery Queen's voice echoed through the chamber, far louder than it had been a moment ago, far louder than any voice could possibly be.

Jack stood and stepped forward to stand by Ivy. "The waters were filled with sludge. The creatures were gasping for air, suffering."

"Lies!" The queen's voice echoed like they were in the ravine, reverberating until Jack's head throbbed. "You dare come before me and tell lies?"

She started coughing again and closed her eyes. Her head drooped.

After one last sneer at them, Ada knelt beside the Faery Queen. "Give me your hand, Mother. I'll deal with them and return the waters to their former state, to what I envision for the folk. You need to rest."

And then Jack understood: Just as Ivy had been helping him when he told a tale to change things, so too had Ada helped the Faery Queen. As he turned to say something to Ivy, he saw the telltale signs of her anger and knew she'd had the same revelation.

"Mother!" Ivy raced to the Faery Queen's side, stumbling at the edge of the dais. "No. The waters were diseased. The folk are suffering. You must believe me. You must listen."

With an awful sound, Ada smacked Ivy, knocking her to the ground and planting a foot on Ivy's throat. "No, Sister. I believe *you* need to listen."

She clutched the Faery Queen's hands and mumbled something Jack couldn't hear.

The Faery Queen looked as if she'd fallen asleep.

Ada twisted her foot on Ivy's throat. "I believe I have some guests waiting to meet you, sister."

Before Jack had moved even two steps, Ada closed her eyes and the chamber doors slammed open. With a roll of cold terror, the Hunt entered the room.

As he glanced behind him, he saw the Glaistigs step between the Hunt and the rest of the chamber, shoulders back and weapons drawn.

"Take them," Ada snarled to the Hunt. Her face was a horrible thing as she glared down at Ivy and added, "Trample them, eat them, keep them alive for torment. Whatever. Just take them out of here."

As one, the Glaistigs' spread out to face the Hunt.

Bollynoggins nocked their arrows.

But the ugliness did not began: the Huntsmen bowed their heads.

The one who'd spoken to Jack and Ivy in the hallway dismounted. He stepped forward so he was chest to chest with Ilanya.

Ilanya did not back up.

"My queen?" The Huntsman leaned to the side and asked in that hollow whispering voice, "Is this what you would ask of us?"

The Faery Queen's head was slumped forward, her eyes staring blindly, her thin chest expanding as she drew in rasping breaths.

Jack caught Ivy's gaze, and then he glanced at the insensible Faery Queen.

Ivy looked at the Faery Queen.

And Jack whispered, "As the princess looked at her mother, the Faery Queen woke and remembered all that happened. She remembered and understood the truth in what Ivy had said."

He opened his eyes briefly and saw the Faery Queen stir, saw her looking around her chamber.

Ada did not notice.

Closing his eyes, he added, "As Princess Ivy looked at her mother, the Faery Queen saw both of her daughters truly. She *saw* them and heard their words. The Faery Queen heard the truth. With each heartbeat, she grew stronger, healthier."

Jack stumbled and fell to the floor. He wanted to help Ivy. He wanted to give her the strength to send Ada flying, but that would have to wait.

"The Faery Queen felt her strength flooding back," he said in as strong a voice as he could muster. "She felt . . ."

"What is he doing?" Ada's voice echoed as the Faery Queen had had earlier.

"She felt well again." Jack opened his eyes and saw the Faery Queen watching Ada. Though she had not moved, the Faery Queen was clearly alert now.

"We obey the Faery Queen. You are not our queen." Despite the objection in his words, the Huntsmen drew a pair of cruel looking blades.

Ilanya gripped the Huntsman's wrists.

Huntsmen and Glaistigs copied the deadly movements, raising their own blades and cudgels, spears and fists. The Bog Mother lifted an arm, and the Bollynoggins all drew back their arrows.

"We ask again if this is what the Faery Queen commands." The Huntsman's voice slithered through the room, an almost touchable terror. "She is the Faery Queen's daughter. To harm one's child . . . it is not a thing that should ever be done."

"I make the decisions here," Ada snapped. She scowled at the Huntsmen. "Do I have to do it myself now? I gave you a command. With the Faery Queen's will in my blood and through my flesh, I command you to take them. Now."

Blades fell; arrows shot through the chamber.

"Actually, *I* make the decisions, Ada, or have you forgotten that?" The Faery Queen pulled her hands from Ada's grasp and said, "Stop."

The sounds of metal upon metal and the grunts of pain stopped.

Jack glanced back briefly. A few moments would've been all the longer the battle would've lasted. The Glaistigs had wounded a couple Huntsmen, and arrows jutted from the flesh of a few hounds, but in all the Hunt looked unscathed.

The Bollynoggins were strewn about the chamber like discarded dolls, limbs at odd angles.

Jonquil was already tending wounded Bollynoggins, though the Glaistigs looked far worse. One had a gash on her leg that made it impossible to stand. She was on her knees, a blade in each hand, still ready to battle. Others--including Ilanya, though she still stood--had injuries which made her wound seem minor.

Jack bit his cheek to keep the sounds of horror inside and turned his gaze back to the dais. *If the battle resumes, we'll all die.*

With obvious effort the Faery Queen straightened herself in the throne and looked at her eldest daughter. "I believe you have some questions to answer."

Then the clear-minded, angry queen looked over the room. "Until I say otherwise, you will all stand down."

The Hunt and the Glaistigs bowed their heads to the Faery Queen and lowered their weapons.

Chapter 16: In which the truth is revealed at least

❦

I lanya leaned down. Blood poured down her flank and a bone poked through the skin on her arm, but she was grinning. "Come now, Jack Merry. We've promised to try to keep you safe here."

She scooped him up with her uninjured arm and steadied him on his feet. Then-- half-carrying, half-supporting him--she led him to the center of the Bollynoggins and the Ellyllon who'd stood with him and Ivy.

Beyond them were the Glaistigs.

Ilanya's injuries weren't the worst of them. In those brief moments of battles, the Glaistigs stood like a wall between the Hunt and the tiny fey. A few of the savage cuts the Glaistigs faced could've killed the much tinier Ellyllon and Bollynoggins.

Jack realized that he was surrounded by armed creatures. *He* was protected, but Ivy was alone with Ada and the Faery Queen. The three stood on the dais.

"You need to help Ivy," he told the creatures all around him.

Trying to steady himself, Jack braced his feet as he'd seen Ivy do when she fought. It helped a little. He tried to shove Ilanya toward them. "Go on."

"Tsk, tsk, tsk, mortal. Shoving me?" Ilanya shook her finger at him, grinning all the while. "Once we'd have drowned a mortal for that kind of rudeness."

He blinked several times, fighting an exhaustion stronger than before. He could see Ivy still on the floor under Ada's foot. Her hair looked like strands of fire snaking across the dark tile, but she still hadn't curled her hand around the hilt of her sword. She looked helpless.

Fine. I'll help her.

He closed his eyes and said, "Ivy looked her sister and . . ."

Ilanya clamped a hand over his mouth and murmured, "Patience."

#

Gingerly, Ivy swallowed. Her throat burned. She turned her head to see the others.

This is when having a real plan would've been good.

With the exception of the terror of the Hunt and the unpredictability of the Glaistigs, Ivy thought things seemed calm. Her strange army looked passably safe. Slowly, she turned her head so she could see her mother.

"Let your sister up, Ada." The Faery Queen's voice resonated in the room. "Now."

Ada lifted her hand as if to strike the Faery Queen. It hung there, an insult but not yet an act of treason.

The Faery Queen lifted one eyebrow.

Ada lowered her hand, but her foot stayed firmly on Ivy's throat.

From behind her, Ivy heard the voice of the Huntsmen from earlier. "Your Queen has spoken, Princess Ada. Shall we enforce her word?"

The Glaistigs stomped their agreement, a thunderous sound in the chamber.

Ada removed her foot.

"My queen." Ivy scrambled to her feet, keeping Ada in sight. "Are you well?"

The Faery Queen laughed, an unpleasant sound that only grew worse in the stillness of the room. When her laughter stopped, she said, "No, daughter, I am not, nor is the realm from what I understand." With anger clear in her voice, she asked, "Were you planning on keeping me like that, Ada? Weak enough that you could use my will?"

Ada shrugged. "I'd thought they'd either assassinate you, or I'd wait it out until you expired." Ada straightened her skirt, hands lost in voluminous folds. "I suppose I should've been more active."

"Indeed," the Faery Queen murmured. She tilted her head, eyes closed, for several breaths as she thought. When she opened them, she asked, "A bit more iron in my drink, perhaps? It was a good plan, all things considered."

"Too late for that now, isn't it?" Ada pulled a small blade from the folds of her skirt. "I am still heir though. If you were to fall . . ."

In the corner of her eye, Ivy could see the Glaistigs moving towards them; they were too far away. She stepped between her sister and her mother and said, "No!"

Lifting her sword, Ivy shook her head. "You will not sit on the throne, Ada."

"Why is that, daughter?" The Faery Queen's voice was low and emotionless.

"I didn't do all this, come this far to see Ada win." Ivy didn't look at her mother. She stared only at her sister.

Ivy thought of the Twitches, the Hound, her lost immortality as she stared steadfastly at her sister.

Then she shook her head. "No."

Still speaking in that low voice, the queen asked, "Why would you protect me?"

"It's not about you," Ivy admitted.

She thought about how best to say it. Now that she knew Ada had been behind the horrible things the folk had endured, she was certain that her mother must stay on the throne. The alternative—Ada in charge, truly wielding the power she'd only borrowed thus far—was unacceptable.

So, Ivy simply said, "Ada would not serve the realm. She *has not* done so."

"Do *you* want to rule, then? Do you want to extinguish your sister's lifespark and take her place as heir?" The Faery Queen sounded curious, not yet angry even though her eldest daughter had tried to kill her and still stood threatening her. "Shall I let you make that choice, Ivy?"

She whispered, "No."

Ada muttered, "You were always too soft to rule. "

Tightening her grip on the sword, Ivy lifted it ever-so-slightly, hoping she looked threatening.

In a louder voice, Ivy added, "But if my Queen wills it, I would extinguish her spark. It's better than the alternative."

\#

Jack listened as the Faery Queen and Ivy carelessly discussed death and assassination.

How did one determine if the Faery Queen was mad or just faery-cruel?

He'd thought she was better, and the depth of what it took out of him to speak those few words, to will the sickness from her, had left him more exhausted than anything he'd done before. She must have been nearing death that her healing exhausting him so fully.

He leaned against Ilanya, still barely able to support himself.

"You haven't much strength left in you," Ilanya said. Her hand still covered his mouth. "No more making things *Change* for you. Eyes open or mouth closed. I will not have you injuring yourself on my watch. Understood?"

He nodded, and Ilanya uncovered his mouth.

"Is she safe there?" he whispered.

"Aaah, the mortal speaks." The Faery Queen's voice carried over the room like a chilling breeze.

When she turned that calculating gaze on him, he wondered if he'd have had the courage to come against her if he'd met her before today. Even though she was frail enough that she looked like a bundle of twigs on the throne, the Faery Queen was more intimidating than the entire Hunt had been.

"Your majesty." Jack bowed his head and hoped kneeling wasn't required. He was fairly certain that he'd end up falling on his face if he tried to kneel.

The queen beckoned with her bony fingers. "Come closer, mortal."

Beside her, the two princesses continued to exchange hostile looks, weapons in hand. They had not--thus far--exchanged blows.

The Faery Queen, however, seemed utterly nonplussed by it.

"My Queen." The Huntsman with the dark mask strode forward. "If I may?"

The Faery Queen shrugged, but her mouth curved in a small smile that the Huntsman took as assent.

As the Huntsman approached, Ilanya released his arm and said, "Go on."

Jack tried not to shudder, but his skin felt cold enough to burn as the Huntsman wrapped cold fingers around his arm and led him closer to the Faery Queen.

Pulling Jack down beside him, the Huntsman knelt at the foot of the dais. His dark armor seemed dull against the glistening black tile, as if it was a shadow in an already dark sky.

Jack swayed, and for a moment thought he'd end up face down on the floor, but the Huntsman steadied him, pulling him closer.

So, Jack leant against that shadowy armor and tried to focus his eyes.

The Faery Queen pushed herself out of her throne and came to stand in front of him. "Mortals are not welcome in my realm."

"I know," he answered, looking up at her briefly. "Ivy told me."
Beside him, the Huntsman tensed.

"Then why, are you here?" the Faery Queen asked.

"Ivy said you were sick.

"I was," the Faery Queen allowed. She glared briefly at Ada.

"My stories become real here," Jack explained. "So, Ivy wanted
us to make you healthy again. I made her sword. I cleaned up the
water for the water-maidens." He looked up at Ivy, still standing in
front of Ada as if they were frozen in place. "I gave her my vow."

The Faery Queen reached out and gripped his chin. She tilted
his head so he looked at her, falling into eyes that could've been
Ivy's if they weren't so forbidding.

"This morning I'd have given you to the Hunt or the Twitches,
but the last of the Twitches are afraid of you, aren't they? And the
Hunt is loath to harm you." The Faery Queen stroked his hair,
running her thin fingers through his curls. "What shall I do now?"

Is this a question I'm to answer?

He waited, hoping for a cue if some sort.

Then the Faery Queen turned to stare at the Huntsman.
"Shall I tell him *why* you seek to protect him?" She bent forward
and whispered in Jack's ear, "Ada sent the Hunt after *her* when
they realized she'd seen the horses--some mortals can, you know.
It's more fun to chase when the prey sees you."

The Huntsman was a Huntswoman?

He tried to turn his head, but the Faery Queen's grip on his
curls held him fast.

"She was a terrible beauty when she lost her child, ready to
destroy everything she could see. When she escaped the Hunt--
clever mortal that she was--she went to the tree where she'd left
her child, her son," the Faery Queen's bony continued. "She raged
so that the fiercest of the folk trembled. That rage and sorrow
called the Hunt to her, recognizing it as their own, and they took
her. But she has made them her own. She is that which sets even
the Hunt to quaking."

The Faery Queen leaned down and kissed his forehead.

"I didn't watch my daughters as carefully as she did," the queen added. "I will watch them as surely as your mother watches you."

Then she let go of him and turned to the Huntswoman. "You've served the realm well. Will you ride out or wait on him?"

The Huntswoman turned to Jack, and in that whispering voice, she asked, "What would you have us do, son?"

He wasn't sure what to say, to do. These creatures were the terror of the realm, and his *mother* led them?

The Faery Queen and the Huntswoman--his mother?--were both staring at him.

Is she truly my mother? Do I want her to stay if she is?

He thought of what Ivy had told him about that night when she'd found him, about his mother's sorrow, and then about what she'd done just now.

He looked at the Faery Queen. "She is your mother, Jack Merry."

My mother. *I have a mother.*

Although his voice was shaking, he said, "Wait, please . . . mother."

\#

Slowly, the Faery Queen approached Ivy and Ada.

Ivy's sword arm was grown heavy, but she stayed as she was--facing her sister in defense of the queen.

"So, what have we decided?" The Faery Queen sounded cheerful, as calm as she'd been in Ivy's earliest memories. A smile had always been ready on the queen's face, no matter what troubles beset the realm.

"Your majesty?" Ivy said, hoping she was misunderstanding.

"What would you do with your sister?" the queen said, speaking each word calmly.

"You are the queen," Ivy murmured, relieved to hear her

mother sound as she had before Ada's apparent attempt at taking the throne.

Everything is going to be fine now.

Ivy looked at the Faery Queen and said, "It is not my place to decide. You rule here."

And that's when Ada lunged. She caught Ivy's side with the tip of her blade, and Ivy felt the metal sink into flesh.

They was too close for Ivy to swing the sword, so she gripped Ada's wrist with her free hand and using her body as leverage, pulled her sister to the ground. Once Ivy's shoulders hit the tile, she rolled them both.

This time Ada was the one pinned down.

The Faery Queen picked up both Ada's dagger and Ivy's sword. "Suggestions, Ivy?"

"Banished a while?" Ivy's side burnt were the cold steel has grazed her skin and her vision began to blur.

Nasty stuff, steel. It must've gone deeper than I thought.

"That's a fine start." Then, the Faery Queen lifted a hand, as calmly as she did everything. "Would you be so kind--Ilanya, is it?"

Ivy heard the Glaistig's hooves as she raced to the Faery Queen's side. "It is."

"I believe Ada needs . . . supervised while my new heir rests. Perhaps later we can discuss security for the palace and, of course, for Ivy and Jack?"

"If Matriarch Sezja can spare our presence, it would be an honour, your grace," Ilanya said

No! What is she doing? Ivy hoped she misunderstood her mother. *Heir?*

"I have her, Princess. I have her." Ilanya pried Ivy's nearly numb fingers free. "Release."

Ivy shook her head. Darkness threatened at the edges of the room, as if Ivy's eyes were determined to close no matter what she wanted.

I cannot pass out!

"Your mother is safe," Ilanya whispered. "We all are now."

Ivy tried to stand to face the Faery Queen, to ask her to repeat herself, but instead she tumbled to the ground and everything went completely dark.

Chapter 17: In which punishment and praise is pondered

✦❦✦

J ack sat in a small antechamber to Ivy's room. He'd slept enough that he was finally clear-headed—or, at least, as clear-headed as he could be with the magic he'd seen. He had faced foes, and he'd helped to save the Faery Queen.

And I have a mother.

Now, he just waited.

Glaistigs and Bollynoggins were curled on the floor between him and the door that led to the rest of the palace. The Bog Mother was in the center of a pile of sleeping Bollynoggins, some still wounded. Only the worst injured had accepts healing. They all wanted to keep their small scars from the fight—which they were trying to name. Apparently, things were better with the right name.

Many of the Glaistigs also slept, but a few stayed alert. Some were watching the tall windows, and others were watching the door. Now that the Faery Queen was better, and Ada was contained somewhere, Jack had thought they'd be safe. But from the postures of the others, he wondered if he was wrong.

He'd been thinking since he'd awakened, questions he couldn't answer: would his mother return above-ground with him? Would he be going above-ground?

What do I want to happen?

The questions swirled in an endless loop.

He stood and paced, looking at Ivy's room. It was the first thing he'd seen that came close to what he'd have imagined. It was like the woods had followed her home and moved inside the palace.

The floor seemed as if it were clear, like ice, but he saw nothing beyond it when he looked at it. The walls were wooden, but not cut wood. They looked like trees had pressed close together, and when he'd touched the leaves that drooped from them, he knew they were real. If not for the windows and the stone-grey door, he'd have believed they were outside.

Further into the room a tree grew from that clear floor; it curved backwards in a serpentine shape, then straightened and continued on into the ceiling. Layers of something white and delicate were piled upon the curve of it, making a bed of sorts in the middle of the trunk. Hanging like a curtain around it were long thin branches, swaying as if a light wind blew through the room.

Ivy slept behind that leafy curtain, like the winged creature she was.

And in a nest above her, the Ellyllon rested.

After they'd brought Ivy here, Jonquil had healed her wound, but she hadn't woken. A healer had come and poured some sweet drink into Ivy's mouth. Still, she'd slept.

The heir to the throne of Faery was napping like a butterfly in a cocoon.

The Faery Queen had sent word that they were to join her for a meal when Ivy woke. The Glaistigs debated who was well enough to escort them.

Still, Ivy slept.

Jack sat down next to the bed, leaning against the tree, and waited. There really was not much else he could do. He wasn't going to leave Faery without seeing her to say goodbye, and he wasn't even sure he wanted to leave at all.

For more than an hour, Jack kept waiting--listening to the steady toll of bells that told him Ivy grew stronger as she slept.

Then, he heard her whisper, "Jack?"

He smiled and moved so he could see her better.

The branches that formed a curtain around her curled up, like small serpents writhing, until they lifted and were tucked away behind a gnarled branch.

"Is everyone safe?" She rolled on to her side and propped herself up with one arm.

"A few of the Glaistigs are pretty cut up, but everyone seems to be well. Better than any of us expected, I think," Jack assured her.

"Why didn't Jonquil heal them?" Her forehead furrowed. Then she glanced up at the nest where the Ellyllon were sleeping. Her voice grew a bit louder. "Is she hurt?"

"No, just exhausted. She healed the worst wounds, and the palace healers came in with bandages and draughts of some sort." He pointed to the others in the antechamber. "The Bollynoggins are sleeping out there, and some of the Glaistigs too."

She nodded; then, she bit her lip. Finally, she whispered, "Did the queen say what would happen to Ada? To us?"

He shook his head. "Not really . . . except that she keeps calling you her heir."

"So that wasn't a bad dream, hmm?" Ivy's eyes were wide, and she bit down on her lip again.

"She took Ilanya with her after we came here. Wants her to go over 'security issues' for the palace." Remembering the gleeful look on Ilanya's face, despite the bruises and blood, he almost smiled. "Ilanya seemed excited."

"She'll have more chances for battles." Ivy shrugged, as if that made perfect sense.

Jack tried to keep his voice even as he said, "And she offered the Hunt a boon of their choice 'should their choice be acceptable to her.'"

Ivy snorted when he said that. Then, she swung her feet to the ground beside him.

He wasn't sure how much Ivy's heard before she fell, so he added, "My mother was pleased."

The word felt funny in his mouth. *Mother. My mother.*

He added, "She said she's waiting until after we speak to the queen before she makes her request."

"Your mother?" Ivy repeated. "She's here? When? How?"

Breathing deeply, Jack said, "She met us in the hallway before we talked to the Faery Queen." He looked at her, afraid of what she'd say. His mother led the things that terrified Ivy, terrified most folk.

"But there weren't any mortals there. Only the Hhh. . ." Ivy's eyes widened, and her mouth hung open. "Your *mother* rides with the *Hunt*?"

When he nodded, she gasped. "Oh, Jack Merry, I'm so sorry. I thought I was rescuing you that night. So that mortal had stolen you? I kept you hidden from your mother?"

She slid down her tree-bed to sit beside him.

His words came out inn a great spill: "No. That was my mother you saw, but she got away. When she couldn't find me, I guess she went a little mad herself and . . . well, she joined the Hunt. She leads them now, that's how she knew I was alive. She saw me, heard the stories. But she didn't come back for me, she didn't bring me here or anything when she found out I was alive."

He felt Ivy's fingers entwine around his.

"It's not been a good place to be, and the Hunt has had to answer to Ada." Ivy squeezed, gently, and added, "Maybe she was afraid?"

Jack felt hope spark in his heart.

"Maybe." He had questions for Ivy-- about what the Hunt had done, why they did it, but he wasn't sure he wanted to know.

Things are different here, he reminded himself. *Do I want to know that my mother is a monster?*

Then Jack looked at Ivy. If anyone understood terrifying mothers, it was Ivy.

Finally, a Glaistig stepped up. "The Faery Queen is waiting for you, Princess."

\#

Ivy kept her back straight as she walked down the hall to the Faery Queen's private dining room. She'd thought about changing out of her stained clothes, but keeping the Faery Queen waiting longer than necessary was rarely a good idea, and reminding her that she and Jack were wounded in service to the realm wasn't a bad plan, either.

Several Glaistigs walked in front of them; others walked behind them.

Ilanya waited at the door. She bowed as they approached. "Princess."

"The queen summoned us?" Ivy despised court protocol, the empty phrasing, the falseness of it all. She'd be on her way out of the palace already if the Faery Queen hadn't summoned them.

If the queen said all was well and left it at that, Ivy was headed back out the palace. Somehow, Ivy doubted that her hopes were about to be answered.

Ilanya leaned in and whispered, "She has left your sister in my herd's care until sentence is pronounced."

Ivy nodded.

Less information is better, right now. Later, perhaps I will want to know . . .

Jack winced, but he didn't ask what kind of care Ada was receiving.

Then, Ilanya opened the door and ushered them in. "Your guests."

The Faery Queen looked infinitely better, almost youthful in comparison to her appearance when Ivy had passed out. The Faery Queen was still unhealthily thin, but her movements were closer to that fluid grace she'd once had, before she'd begun to grow ill.

The door closed. No one else was in the chamber, just the three of them.

"Daughter." The Faery Queen motioned them to the small table.

"Mother," Ivy managed to say, sounding mostly steady.

"Your majesty," Jack said.

They sat.

Once, many years ago, she and Ada had dined here with the Faery Queen. They had been a family, but Ivy had grown older, become a teenager, wanted to explore the realm. A trickle of guilt wriggled through her.

Would I have noticed sooner?

If she'd stayed here when her mother began to grow ill, would Ivy have been able to protect the Faery Queen? Would Ada have been able to poison their mother so easily? If she'd tried to understand her mother's erratic choices, would the madness have lasted so very long?

Is it my fault for staying away so much?

"I'm pleased that you're both well." The Faery Queen lifted a thin-stemmed glass and peered into it with a wry smile. "Ada used to bring me my drink. I didn't bother to have it tasted, not from my daughter's hand. Foolish of me, I see."

She lifted it to her lips and drank deeply.

"Everything here was tested by the Glaistigs before the door was closed. You'll be safe," she announced.

Ivy nodded.

"Eat, children." The Faery Queen waved towards the food, trays of succulent meats and cold fruit.

Once they obeyed, the room was silent but for the sounds of

dishes and occasional tap as a goblet was lowered the table after drinking.

Finally, the queen said, "I am surprised that you'd take such risks for me, Ivy."

Silently, Jack picked up a cluster of honeyed winter plums.

"The realm was in pain." Ivy lifted her own glass, her mouth suddenly dry. "I should've done more sooner. . . When you first became unwell, I didn't realize it was a sickness. I thought you were simply growing crueler."

"A reasonable thought," the Faery Queen murmured. "Ada surely counted on it. We've never been close; have we, Ivy?"

"No."

"I believe we should change that." The Faery Queen smiled, and it was almost a pleasant smile. "If you're to take the throne someday, it'd be foolish to stay so unaware of one another."

Pausing to weigh her words, Ivy tried to think of how to answer her mother without angering her. There weren't any. So, she settled on, "I will be a better daughter. Visit more. See you more."

"Good." Her mother nodded. "Do not feel guilt, Ivy. Children grow. It's what we want—to raise strong, independent daughters. I did that."

"If I'd been home—"

"Nonsense," the Faery Queen said loudly. "I didn't stay home when I was finally old enough to see the world. These are my subjects, and I traveled to meet all of them—and mortals, too."

She paused and smiled at Jack.

Then, her entire body seemed to become regal. She sounded less like a mother and more like a queen. "In putting the realm first, you did what needed to be done, Ivy."

Ivy rolled words around in her mind, hoping for an answer that wasn't 'and now I'm an heir.' Ada clearly couldn't rule, but being queen was not what she'd wanted.

Not ever.

"Would you sacrifice them now?" the Faery Queen continued. "Your Ellyllon? The Bog Mother and her brood? The folk you saw on your trip? Will you leave them and all the rest without a queen?" The Faery Queen caught and held Ivy's gaze. "After what you've done, would you let the realm fall when I can no longer rule? What will happen when I die?"

Die?

"I'm not going to be here long enough." Ivy almost cheered at the realization, however grim, that *she* would die before the immortal queen was ready to pass over rule of the realm.

Ivy sat up straighter. "I've bound myself to Jack Merry. He's a mortal, mother. I'll fade when he dies."

"I see." The Faery Queen turned her wily gaze on Jack. "Your life tied to hers: would you ask me to un-do this? A *boon* for what you've done, perhaps?"

"No!" Ivy exclaimed.

As the Faery Queen peered at him, Jack looked helplessly back at her, like a trapped thing, but he didn't answer.

"It's done." Ivy looked at her mother. "It is the way of it, Mother. Your rule. I have done this, and so I must abide by it. 'Royals are not immune from the law.' You said that."

"And if I should simply undo the rule?" The Faery Queen nibbled a berry and then added, "You are my chosen heir now; being plagued with mortality would not serve the realm."

"I am bound to Jack Merry," Ivy insisted.

"So be it." The Faery Queen lifted her voice then, "I give you a gift, Jack Merry, for your service to my people. Your bond to Princess Ivy shall stand, but it is *her* lifespark that shall determine your shared lifetime, not the reverse."

As she spoke, Jack's eyes widened, and he looked around. After a moment, he said, "I can't hear the bells. They've stopped ringing. Does that mean she's immortal again?"

"Yes," the Faery Queen said.

"*Neither* of us are mortal now," Ivy whispered. She was happy for Jack, but now she had no valid way to refuse her mother.

"I'm fine with not being immortal. I'd never thought of wanting that, but Ivy"--he sighed and stared at her--"I wasn't fine with you giving it up. I know you don't want to be queen, but she's not talking about taking over *right now*, is she?"

He looked at the Faery Queen.

The Faery Queen shook her head, looking as content as Kayt did when he found a wide sunbeam. The Faery Queen had them exactly where she wanted, as she wanted. She was visibly content.

"Maybe there'll be a way around it. We'll have time to figure it out," Jack continued. "You did rescue the Faery Queen, you know?"

"A way around it, indeed," the Faery Queen scoffed and shook her head. "It's not a punishment, Ivy."

Ivy sighed.

Trapped in a palace, pointless protocol, meting out punishments. Why would anyone want such a job?

"Will I still be allowed to travel?" she asked the Faery Queen.

"With your guards or with Jack Merry, if he chooses to stay. I'm quite sure his mother will arrange guards for him now that the Hunt is free of Ada's whims."

"I am your heir, then," Ivy said morosely.

"You are," the Faery Queen said. She lifted a delicate-looking napkin and patted her lips. Then, she smiled coldly and said, "Now that we've tended to that detail, there's Ada's treason to address."

\#

Jack didn't see why he needed to go to the throne room with Ivy and the Faery Queen, but they'd insisted, and in truth he wasn't sure what else to do.

Immortality. A mother.

H e no longer had to return above-ground if he wanted to stay.

Do I want to stay?

As Ilanya escorted Ada into the room, the Faery Queen motioned for Ivy to stand beside her on the dais. Then, the queen looked at Jack Merry expectantly.

Me?

"Go on, Jack," Ilanya urged. "You've as much right as Ivy to stand there today."

Mutely, he went to stand by Ivy.

Several Huntsmen, including his mother, stood in the room. The Bog Mother and her guards entered behind them. After them, others--most of whom he'd never seen--pressed into the room.

None too gently, Ilanya and another Glaistig pushed Ada to her knees.

The Faery Queen frowned at her eldest daughter and said, "If I were as cruel as your sister fears, I'd have you executed. You do know that, don't you?"

Ada nodded. She looked almost as defiant as she had when she stood on the dais, ordering the Hunt to trample them.

"In ruling the folk, with long memories and longer lives, true punishment must be a lengthy thing, or a final act. I still belief that change is possible if there is time." The Faery Queen reached out to grab Ivy's hand. "Princess Ivy will rule the folk. You will not rule, Ada.Not ever. Not even if I die and your sister dies."

The Faery Queen stared out at the assembled crowd.

No one spoke.

"Time. Time for us to change and to heal is what we need now." The Faery Queen's voice grew louder, so clear and crisp thay even those in the back could surely hear as clearly as if they stood next to the queen. "Hopefully, in time, you will consider the error in what you've done."

"My Queen?" Ivy spoke up, apparently pleasing the Faery Queen for she smiled almost lovingly. "If Ada is to be banished, how can we assure that she'll not return home without our permission?"

"Our permission?" The Faery Queen quirked one corner of her mouth.

"Yes, Mother, *ours*. If I'm stuck being the heir, I am accepting the duties that means."

The Faery Queen's smile grew.

"Until we both agree that she's no longer a threat to our people, I believe she should be left *above-ground*." Ivy stared at Ada as she spoke.

"Certainly." The Faery Queen stood and released Ivy's hand. She walked over to Ada. "But that is not enough, now is it, Ada? Ivy thinks of the good of the realm; she thinks of how to keep us safe down here. I must also think of their suffering while I was ill."

She stroked Ada's hair, lovingly despite what she must do. The queen pronounce, "While you walk there, surrounded by mortals, without a servant, your voice shall be silenced."

She rested her fingers on Ada's throat and when she pulled her hand away, something living and fibrous was in her hand.

Ada's mouth moved as if she spoke, but no sound came out: The Faery Queen had taken her voice.

The Faery Queen took that fibrous mass and twisted it in her hand. Then she looped it around Ada's neck. As she did so, it changed so it looked like a solid metal circlet, on the top of it was a grey band.

Mouth moving soundlessly, Ada reached up to touch the circlet; her fingers reddened and bled.

And Jack knew then what it was--a thin line of steel, the same poisonous metal as Ivy's sword blade.

The Faery Queen pulled Ada to her feet.

"You claimed to speak for me," the queen said. "You lied and ordered things that hurt my realm. You fed me cold steel to keep me weak, to control me." She ran a finger over that grey line and held it up so everyone could see the blood that dripped from it. "As long as you wear this, you'll be weak. To remove it, you would need to cut it, and if you do that, I'll not be able to return it to your throat. Your voice will be gone permanently." Then she kissed Ada on both cheeks. "May you learn quickly."

Epilogue: in which Jack and Ivy visit the Ellyllon

True to her word, the Faery Queen allowed Ivy to roam. She'd been above-ground with Jack to visit the Widow--and to stop to talk to Arth for a while. Keeping an eye on what happened above-ground was a priority to Ivy and to the Faery Queen now that Ada was living there.

And Ivy had ridden with the Hunt--not for pursuit of anyone, but just to feel the thrill of moving that quickly. It wasn't something she'd ever considered, but when Jack asked her to go, she'd heard the worry in his voice. He'd been learning to spend time with his mother, but it was still far from comfortable. Not that her own time with her own mother was comfortable either.

They were both learning.

The Huntswoman offered Jack one of the steeds whenever he wanted, but so far, he only went when he could share a steed with Ivy.

However, Jack's mother was cautious, eager to keep her son safe, so Jack and Lily both had at least one hound with them, often the one they'd met in the meadow. It was a fair trade, though, better than staying close to the palace or traipsing around with Ilanya in tow.

Today, Jack leaned forward and asked in a low voice, "Are we almost there?"

Even if he did accept a steed, Ivy would still need to go with him. He hadn't developed much of a sense of direction.

"Close," she whispered.

Last time they'd visited the Bog, the Bollynoggins had showered them with swamp water upon arrival. Clematis had led the charge.

Ivy hadn't given up on finding a way around the burden of ruling, but as Jack reminded her, "We have almost eternity to figure it out."

"Psst, Ivy, Jack." Jonquil peeked out from between a few leaves. She pointed to a large boulder along the path.

"Close your eyes and hold on, Jack Merry." Ivy urged her water-horse forward so she could see Clematis and the hidden Bollynoggins. "Now. Say it now!"

Eyes closed, Jack said, "And Ivy saw that the little trouble-makers were all caught in a puddle of honey, utterly unable to move their feet."

Then, he opened his eyes and grinned at the squirming Bollynoggins.

"Who warned you?" Clematis frowned at her sticky wings. "Just wait."

She turned to a Bollynoggin beside her. "I told you we should've bound his mouth first. But, no. No one listens to my strategy. Hpmph."

Ivy giggled. They were all a terrible mess.

The Bog Mother and her guards rounded the corner. "Princess. Jack. Glad you could come for the announcement." Then she looked at her boys, who were now throwing globs of honey at each other and at Jack and Ivy. "I was going to wait until later, but I think now seems like a fine time. They're all yours, Daisy."

Clematis gaped at her sister.

Grinning, Jack slipped down from the horse and sat on the ground beside Daisy. "I thought you said you were done with watching out for troublemakers."

Blushing, Daisy muttered, "Hagan and I . . . well, I'm staying here and . . . I already have plenty of practice looking out for trouble makers. I will be the next Bog Mother."

Grandmother Nogs winked at Ivy. "My regards to the queen, Ivy." And to Jack, "Jonquil's finished the salve your mother wanted. Let me know if this one works better at offsetting the terror when you ride."

"I will." Jack nodded, laughing as a shower of honey pelted him. Several Bollynoggins had worked themselves free and crept up alongside him.

Things weren't quite as they'd been in the tales Jack used to tell above-ground, but they were far finer than Ivy had dared believe possible when she'd brought Jack Merry home.

For now, that's enough.

About the Author

Melissa Marr is a former university literature instructor who writes fiction for adults, teens, and children. Her books have been translated into twenty-eight languages and have been bestsellers internationally (Germany, France, Sweden, et. al.) as well as domestically.

Fourteen years ago, she wrote her first book—*this one*—aloud, for her kids. Since then, she's written more than 17 novels, toured in almost every state, as well as several countries. More importantly, she adopted two more kids and moved to four more states. In the middle of that, every year, she has gone back to this book and revised. This year, it seemed like it was worth reading.

＆

Praise for Melissa Marr's Books:
On *WICKED LOVELY*

"Marr's fantasy world is complex and involving." — *The New York Times*

"Enticing...Marr creates a fully realized world... The suspense remains taut...The romantic scenes are delicious...Marr's lyrical language and sensual imagery capture both the confused emotions and the physicality of adolescence." —*Washington Post*

"A fully imagined faery world that even non-fantasy (or faeriey) lovers will want to delve into."– *Publishers Weekly*, STARRED REVIEW

"Marr's first novel exemplifies urban fantasy... readers are rewarded with a ripping climax that leaves us keen for the next book." — *Cleveland Plain Dealer*

"For once, a girl in a supernatural series doesn't need to be saved by a burly, immortal dude in her life. In this one, human chick [Aislinn] is no damsel in distress. She packs a wallop of her own... [while] discovering her true raison d'etre." — *The New York Post*

"This dark fantasy about survival and transformation is as mesmerizing as its urban faery subjects." — *Booklist*

"The unusual combination of past legends and modern-day life gives a unique twist to this "fairy" tale." — *School Library Journal*

On CARNIVAL OF SECRETS (originally published as Carnival of Souls):

"Lives collide in a spectacular tangle of love, hate, and long-standing vendettas...Add in class warfare, a deadly tournament, and the Carnival of Souls, where any pleasure or contract can be fulfilled, and this is one novel that will be at the top of everyone's to-read list." —*Voice of Youth Advocates* (starred review).

"Marr showcases her impressive talent by crafting an incredible, fantastical, complex world. This book is worth reading for the amazing fight scenes alone."--*RT Book Reviews* (TOP PICK)

"Marr's trademark blend of dark romance, fantasy, and action is on full display." —*Publisher's Weekly*

On SEVEN BLACK DIAMONDS:

"Once again, Marr has built an urban fantasy world that readers will find irresistible."-- *School Library Journal*

"A compelling world of magic, power, and regret."-- *Bulletin of the Center for Children's Books*

"Marr's trademark use of suspense and romance will make this irresistible for her legions of fans."-- *Booklist*

facebook.com/MelissaMarrBooks

twitter.com/melissa_marr

goodreads.com/melissa_marr

Also by Melissa Marr